GELSY 2

DAVEY AND GELSY

DANNI BAYLES-YEAGER

Order this book online at www.trafford.com
or email orders@trafford.com

Most Trafford titles are also available at major online book retailers.

Printed in the United States of America.

ISBN: 978-1-4907-5249-5 (sc)
ISBN: 978-1-4907-5250-1 (e)

Library of Congress Control Number: 2015900926

Trafford rev. 01/20/2015

www.trafford.com

North America & international
toll-free: 1 888 232 4444 (USA & Canada)
fax: 812 355 4082

Dedicated to

Leonard Nimoy

for

Baffled!

CHAPTER 1

"Are all honeymoons this fantastic, my darling Davey?" Gelsy was wrapped in a huge beach towel and propped up against her new husband's chest as they reclined back against a piece of driftwood.

"You're asking the wrong guy, honey. This is my first one, but I know nothing can top it." David chuckled. "Just having you out of the hospital in one piece is enough to make it pretty special. You keep trying to convince me you're my wife, and I might think I'm having some kind of hallucination." He bent down to kiss her cheek and forehead.

"Tell me, what did the doctor say to you when he checked me out this morning, just before we had the wedding in the chapel?" She'd lifted herself up on one hand so she could turn and look into his face.

"Gelsy, he's only sincerely worried about you . . ."

"Aha! I was right. He did try to warn you against making love, didn't he?"

He took her face in both his hands and looked at her sadly. "My dearest girl, you were in a terrible car accident. It took both your parents and left you nearly dead. It was a real miracle I got you back, Gelsy, so I'm not taking any chances. The doctor says it still may be a long time until you're completely recovered."

"Darling, my broken leg is healed enough for me to walk without a crutch, my broken ribs seem to be fine, all the stitches are out, and my only problem will be a broken heart if my Davey says that we cannot love each other now that we're finally man and wife."

He brushed the hair back from her face. The sea breeze had come up with the rising tide, and she always forgot to tie back her Rapunzel-like head of hair. "My dearest . . . wife. Good god, how can I ever get used to saying that, Gelsy? It rips my heart out just to look at you and think you belong to me now." He pulled her in to his chest and put her head on his shoulder. "But if you're going to be mine, you can be damned sure I'm going to take the very best care of you I can. They're worried about bones re-breaking and possibly damaging your internal organs? That's all I need to hear. I'm going to handle you like you were made of porcelain."

Gelsy said nothing; she snuggled in as close to him as possible, running her hands over his shirt and pulling her face back for a kiss. David vowed resolutely it would be a chaste kiss and then he'd get her settled in a bed of her own so she could rest after the trip, but she obviously had other ideas. Unbuttoning his shirt in four seconds flat, she reached inside and ran her hands around his chest. Lowering her head, she began kissing these areas while her hands became busy with areas further down.

"Whoa, girl!" The new husband was amused and excited but determined to stick to his promise to her doctors. "It's great to know you still have a yen for me after all that's happened, but let's go slow, OK? Gelsy? Unzipping my jeans is not what I call 'going slow' . . ."

He had a lot of other things to say, like the fact they were outside a bed-and-breakfast inn on the beach with the tide rising or that it was a public area and anybody might decide to walk by their little secluded strip of driftwood-covered land at any time. Lots of things he should have said, but by this time she had managed to take his mind off every one of them. The weeks she'd spent in the hospital were miserably lonely ones for him, accustomed as he was to sharing her bedroom three or four nights a week before.

He'd told their friend Gordie once that heroin was the only thing that came close to the thrill of sleeping with a woman you truly loved, and the withdrawal had been hard on him.

She had taken control and stretched herself across his body. *I'm not putting any weight on her*, David thought. *Hopefully, I can't hurt her like this.* She was wearing only a little beach shift, which was why they needed to borrow the big towel before walking down to the breakers. David slid down onto his back and pulled the towel over her. Reaching up under her dress he realized that somehow she'd already been able to lose her underwear. *How does she do that?* he wondered, and then there was no more room for thoughts in his head—only the terrible joy that mating with her always brought him, making him feel invincible and yet, at the same time, adding to the fear that someday, in some way, he might lose her.

"Davey?" Her voice seemed to drift to him from a long way away, through the sound of the shore-breaking waves and across the soft darkness he was resting in after feeling such intense pleasure.

Without opening his eyes he responded, "What is it, you little sex manic, you?" And he braced himself for her attack.

"Oh! What a horrible thing to say to your bride on your wedding day! And just because she's been pining away for you all this time. Just for that, I *shall* sleep alone for the rest of the trip!"

Her two little fists were thumping his sides, more like an Oriental massage than a beating.

"We *shall* see about that," he said, laughing as he rolled over and pinned her gently in the sand. "After that demonstration, I don't know if I'm as brave as I thought I was. I think I'm just going to have to pray very hard and be very careful, my darling girl."

She calmed down immediately and gave him her biggest smile. "My love, let's have a happy honeymoon, even if it is only for a few days because of winter quarter starting."

"Poor Gelsy, you got cheated out of a big wedding like you always dreamed about, and now you only have a four-day honeymoon. You deserved a trip to the Grecian Isles at least."

"Well, maybe next summer we can go there, if you wish. You know I couldn't have the big wedding without Mama and Papa there, and I was perfectly happy with the wedding we had. Everyone dear to us was there, and you looked so handsome!"

"And when I saw you in your Juliet dress again, it nearly broke my heart, girl." He kissed her eyelids. "I remembered how beautiful you looked onstage that night, and how you ran to me backstage after it was over."

"Well, I'm glad you got to see me dance that night, darling, because who knows if I'll ever be able to perform again?" She suddenly became very serious. "Maybe I'll only get well enough to be able to teach someday. But that would be OK, you know."

He adjusted his clothing and got to his feet. Holding a hand down for her, he said, "I promised God that if he gave you back to me in any shape whatsoever, I'd be happy, Gelsy."

She took his hand and stood, looking up into his eyes. "You promised God that? Really, Davey?"

"Yes, really. If I had to carry you everywhere, if you were blind and I had to read to you, it didn't matter. I just wanted you in my life, girl. You are my life, now." And he pulled her in close. "Remember, you told me one time not to go anywhere without you. Well, you're not allowed to go anywhere without me, either." He put his lips on hers to seal the bargain.

Walking back to the inn, their arms wrapped around each other's backs, they talked about the car accident that had taken her parents and nearly ended her life, and how David had sworn that night that if she was dead, he would join her. All he would ask was to see her body so he could kiss her one last time, then he would make the run of his life from the hospital to the dorm, where his gun was hidden under his mattress. "I figured it would take me three and a half minutes to make the run, Gelsy, and they said that after they nearly coded you as dead you started breathing again on your own in exactly three and a half minutes!" David stopped for a moment and just looked at her. "Tell me, did you know?"

"I must have. I remember telling Buba that I needed to come back because you had a gun and you were going to use it. He was so upset, poor Buba! All he could say was 'So I would have lost *him*, too'!"

"When we get back, let's call Robert. We're all he's got, now that you're parents are gone."

"He's so proud of you, Davey! All your end-of-quarter grades were perfect, even though you had too much on your mind. And you took his name, then turned around and gave it to me! I don't think any father has ever been prouder of his son than he is of you, my dearest."

"I'd be a sorry excuse of an adopted son if I didn't give your godfather all the credit in the world. Thanks to him I got a doctoral program and the woman I love." And here he laughingly started walking again, pulling her along with him. "Scratch that, adore."

Back at the inn, David asked to have their rooms changed from two twin beds to one king-sized bed; Gelsy was beaming in the background. When they got to their room, they were thrilled to see Victorian-style furnishings and decor mixed with modern-day comfort. The big bed, with its hand made quilts and pillowcases, especially said, "Come cuddle in me."

But a brief call to Robert, assuring him they had arrived safely in Santa Barbara and that "Gelsy was feeling just fine, thank you," came first. Following that was a belated lunch of hot soup and cold sandwiches. Homemade pie for dessert left them both feeling sleepy and thinking maybe a nap would be in order before exploring the evening's entertainment options. Upstairs they trekked one flight of stairs, David all but carrying the tired but determined little dancer. ("How am I going to get well if I let you carry me everywhere?") Once in the room, however, she sank into the bed without protesting.

"Oh, this is so much nicer than a hospital bed!" she sighed. David slipped her sandals off and lovingly rubbed her bare feet before burying them in the quilts. "Thank you, darling."

"You go on to sleep. I want to call Robert again to ask him if he's heard anything more about that World Health conference," David whispered in her ear. Taking the room phone out to the balcony, he closed the sliding glass door and rang Robert's number again.

"I had a feeling you'd call back." The professor was right, as usual. "How's my little girl doing?"

"Really, Robert, she's amazing. Insists on walking everywhere on her own, won't let me carry her, only holds onto my arm when she really needs to. Well, you know what a trooper she is. Right now she's taking a nap after eating a big lunch, so I don't think you have much to be worried about."

"Thank you, my boy. That sets my mind at ease. And now I assume what you want to hear is about the WHO meeting. You did tell Gelsy she's not to mention it to anyone, didn't you?"

"Yes, sir, I told her it was top secret . . . governments may fall, heads might roll, that sort of thing."

"And that's not far from the mark, David. From what I'm hearing lately, it's even worse than we anticipated. The need is more immediate, and the powers that be in that country are more desperate than ever to keep it all under wraps. No one knows how many have died already."

"When are you leaving, sir?"

"It's looking more and more like when are *we* leaving, David. It's an awful thing to thrust on you during your honeymoon, but I don't think I'm going to be able to handle this alone, not with the health problems I've had since . . . well, you know."

David hung his head. Losing Donald and Adele had hit Robert as hard, if not harder, than it hit Gelsy. His heart literally broke, and he wound up in the hospital in critical care for nearly as long as she was there.

"But, Robert, doesn't it mean going into complete seclusion? Kind of like a jury when they're deliberating a case? We might be locked up somewhere in Switzerland for who knows how long, and they don't even let you communicate with the outside world."

"That's all absolutely correct, Son. And it's no way to start off a marriage. If there's any way to get around taking you, I'll do it. But you've got to realize that Gordie and Mark don't have the keys to the work that you have. So much of it is built on what you started in Carmichael, and

I've kept them out of the loop on that by design. I wanted them to work on their sections and get results without knowing what you and I were aiming for so their data wouldn't reflect any wishful thinking."

"I understand that. And you know I'll do whatever you need me to do."

"Well, right now I'd say I want you to get back to your wife and spend what precious little time you have over the next few days making her feel loved. Does that sound too difficult for you?"

David smiled to himself. "It's my favorite thing to do, Robert."

"Good man. Cheerio!" The phone went dead.

David quietly opened and shut the sliding door and replaced the phone, unplugging it first so it wouldn't ring at any inopportune time. Then he stripped down to his underwear and slipped under the covers. Being in a real bed with Gelsy again after all this time, not to mention thoughts of a secret health conference he might have to attend, made him feel so edgy that he had no intentions of napping. Just stretching out next to his girl and relaxing, hearing her breathe, was all he wanted. Strangely enough, once he stretched himself out full-length under the clean sheets his mind immediately started to drift off. He could hear the sound of the ocean waves outside, and they seemed to rock him back and forth.

The next thing he knew, he was lying up against Gelsy like two spoons in a drawer. His left arm was wrapped around her, and she was clutching it; his face was half buried in her hair, and he already had an erection. Just lying there and gently moving against her felt so good, though. He had her back in his arms, and he swore he was never going to let her go again. He'd have to tell Robert there was no way he could leave her to go to Switzerland. Damn, he had a hard enough time leaving her to go buy a newspaper!

By now she was waking up and enjoying the situation she found herself in. Wrapped in his arms, with his manhood pressing against her back, she reveled in his need for her. Reaching behind she stroked him until he began to moan; then she carefully rolled over and slipped out of her shift. Having his beautiful wife naked in his arms, there was no way David could keep the promises to doctors; all he could do was to pray and be as gentle as possible.

Their lovemaking had the same tentative but desperate feeling to it that their very first time, in the back of her car, had been like. When he'd been so unsure of himself but so in need of her. All his experience up to that time had been with prostitutes, and he'd only thought of having sex, never of making love. Then, as now, there had been the fear of hurting her.

Her soft moaning reassured him. He wasn't hurting her, only giving her pleasure. Whenever he thought of that, it always aroused him further. Bringing her pleasure had become as much of a thrill as taking it, and he prided himself on the different ways he'd found to make her happy.

Finally they both lay completely sated and satisfied, laughing about the disobeyed doctors' orders and how "sexual healing" should be a new branch of medicine.

"There's a street fair and a farmer's market going on right now. Want to share a shower and run down to check it out?" Gelsy suggested.

"Sounds good. We can pick up something to keep up here to snack on if we get hungry."

Telling her about the World Health conference would have to wait.

CHAPTER 2

It was on the drive back to campus that David finally worked up the courage to tell her how important, and how secretive, the conference was to be. "Robert thinks he may need me there. You know his heart has been giving him trouble ever since your parents died. He doesn't know if he can handle the strain of a closed conference like that on his own, and nobody else knows the research results, not even Gordie or Mark."

Gelsy frowned. "It's horrible. He's been to special conferences like that, Davey, and sometimes they can take weeks, even months!"

"We have to hope this isn't going to be like that. The country involved is in a bad way. Every week they let go by means hundreds, if not thousands, of their people dying of starvation. They must have the results of our research, even if it means giving up nuclear warheads."

"They're not going to do that easily or quickly, darling. They don't put the same value on human life that you do, remember. They've already sacrificed so many lives just to get nuclear capabilities. I can't see them giving them up without a million provisions in the contract."

"Whatever it means, you must remember never to breathe a word of this to anyone, Gelsy."

"I've been Buba's confidant since I was a child, Davey."

"I know, girl. I'm sorry. I'm just so worried about what all this is going to mean for us. It seems like we've had so much to deal with already. How many newlyweds have gotten off to as rocky a start as we have, anyway?"

"Well, at least we had four lovely days at the beach in Santa Barbara. I'll never forget that, Davey. And I'll always be able to tell our children about how beautiful our honeymoon was!"

There it went again—that pain in his heart he felt whenever she mentioned children. It wasn't that he didn't want them, he did. But for some reason to hear this lovely creature—who he still didn't feel worthy of—talk about having *his* children could wound him like nothing else. Nearly losing her in the accident and then marrying her in the hospital chapel left him with a feeling of tenuousness. This wasn't real, wasn't forever. It was not like a wedding in a real church would have been. She could drift away again at any moment for any number of reasons. Steering with his left hand, he reached out with his right hand for hers and held it fast.

"I still think we should plan a real honeymoon for this summer . . . maybe a long cruise to those Grecian Isles? And maybe a real church wedding before we leave. Wouldn't it be nice to tell those children someday that we really did get married in a church instead of a hospital?"

"If that's what you want, dearest. I'm sure half the UCSM campus would be thrilled to attend this time," she said, grinning.

They reached their home before dark. Robert was already there, having moved in during their absence and made himself at home in Donald's old den. Gelsy and David would stay in her wing, of course, and they would always feel the comforting presence of her parents around them.

"Welcome back!" he called from the doorway. "Nice to have you, not to mention my car, safely home again."

"And without a scratch on it. I even filled the tank at a station just outside town, sir." David gave a smart bow as he handed over the keys.

Gelsy simply threw herself into her godfather's arms and covered his face in kisses. "Thank you so much for the lovely honeymoon, Buba!" she cried. "We were very happy there on the beach, walking on the sand. My leg feels much better from it."

"I'd give you a hard time for letting her overdo it, David, but she's blooming like a rose. So I think it was all for the best. And lord knows she's so headstrong she will have her own way!"

"We agreed on that once before, remember? Looks fragile, really tough as nails," David replied.

"Absolutely right, my boy! Well, young Mrs. Chaveral, since you seem to need something to do to keep you out of trouble, I've brought home a vast array of prepared foods for the hoot tonight, and they're in the kitchen. You may lay them all out on the sideboard. Yes, we will have a hoot tonight, just the three of us, in honor of your family and in honor of you being home safe and sound. It's what they would have wanted."

"As usual, you are so right, my Buba. If Davey doesn't mind taking in the luggage, I will get everything set up in the dining room." Gelsy smiled through a few natural tears and took off like a shot. The two men watched her scurry away.

"I swear, David, you've done wonders for her! She barely has a limp now. No one who saw her today would guess how close to death she was just a few short weeks ago."

"Robert, you can't imagine the amount of praying I've done in those weeks. But having her back beside me these last few days was worth anything. All I can do is thank God now."

"Well, contrary to the doctor's orders, love seems to have been the best medicine after all.

Now, don't you go blushing on me! That woman had a very happy honeymoon."

"Listen, I had a very happy honeymoon. In spite of worrying that you were going to take me off to some top secret conference, away from my new wife the minute after I got back."

"Maybe not the minute after, but close. Does she know?"

"She does. And knows to keep quiet about it."

"Then she will. She always has in the past. I've been on these kinds of trips before, you know."

"So she said. She also said they can take weeks, if not months."

"True. And actually, under the conditions of your scholarship, I could force you to go, but I won't. I'm hoping you'll come with me because we both know how much I'm going to need you there." He put a hand on the tall young man's shoulder.

"You know that goes without saying, Robert. Everything I have now has come because of you. There's no way I could repay you if I spent the rest of my life trying."

"Good lad, my son. Now, put your luggage away and meet us in the dining room."

They separated, David to deposit the suitcases and Robert to help Gelsy in the kitchen, but the new father–son relationship between the two was off to a good start. Robert's adoption papers had only cleared the court with hours to spare when David shared his new name, *Chaveral*, with Gelsy in the hospital chapel. They'd been a family for less than a week.

But when they sat down for dinner together, you'd have thought they'd spent their whole lives in each other's pockets.

The conversation was mainly about the honeymoon, of course. They had chosen the little inn because it had been Donald and Adele's honeymoon spot. "And I'm surprised it's still there," Robert joked, "because the stories Adele told about tearing up the place during their lovemaking were phenomenal!"

Laughing so hard she nearly fell on the floor, Gelsy shot back, "Then I am truly my mother's child, Buba! Davey even had the nerve to call me a sex maniac, and on our wedding day, no less."

David couldn't help laughing but knew he must look like someone had lit a fire under his chin. To cover up the blushing, he stood and offered, "Dessert, anybody?"

"Sit back down, my boy. We can serve ourselves, been doing it for years." Robert was in stitches over his new son's embarrassment. "Gelsy's right, she is truly her mother's daughter. I'm afraid you don't even know the half of what you've let yourself in for!"

David sat back down and tried to act nonchalant. "I promised God if he'd give her back to me in any shape whatsoever, I'd take it without complaining. If this is the worst I have to look forward to, sir, I'll consider myself damned lucky."

"Well said, and exactly what I'd expect a son of mine to say." Robert looked the young man over appreciatively. "Now, what we should spend a little time talking about, if Gelsy doesn't mind, is the conference."

"No, Buba, I am as curious as Davey to know more about this ultrasecret meeting."

"Yes, it is ultrasecret." Robert glanced around the table, almost as if checking for hidden wires. "We must be very careful about what we say and who we say it to. What we can say is that it's a conference of World Health leaders, who are calling on a few specialized researchers to put together a new program. We can't say it's for a troubled country, or anything at all about the research itself."

"When does it begin, Robert?" David was already getting a sinking feeling in the pit of his stomach.

"That's the bad part. It starts a week from today. Everyone is expected to be at the hotel in Switzerland by Thursday night, and total seclusion begins Friday morning. There will be no direct contact with the outside world by anyone connected with the proceedings, and only a brief message to family can be delivered every other night. It, of course, will be scrutinized backward, forward, and sideways to be sure it doesn't contain any coded reference to conference proceedings. My friend from Japan, Dr. Yuki Nori, he's a specialist in Oriental medicine, contacted me today. They do want very much for you to attend, too, David."

The sinking feeling was turning into the feeling of being sucker-punched. How could he leave his girl, his new *wife*, when she'd only been out of the hospital less than a week? David's love for her was greater than almost anything, except maybe his feeling of obligation to one man. Robert was the reason he'd come to UCSM, the person who'd introduced him to Gelsy, and the man who had given him a name to be proud of. He never had to be afraid of being associated with David Collins again. That poor slob had gotten mixed up with a heroin ring in the army when he was trying to recover from the pain of a buddy's death and three nearly lethal tours of duty.

He was now David Chaveral, son of one of America's top biochemists. How do you repay that?

"You know if you need me, I'll be there, Robert." David prayed that came out sounding steady and sincere. Inside he was making a mental note to set up an appointment with his PTSD counselor. Maybe it was time to start considering medication for the stress. *No, they'll be testing everyone at the conference, drug-screening. You don't want to be explaining that.*

He looked across the table at Gelsy. She understood.

CHAPTER 3

Getting ready for bed that night, Gelsy was strangely quiet. As usual, David enjoyed being the first one under the covers. He loved watching her make the final preparations, brushing her hair, putting lotion on her hands and feet. Sometimes he'd order her to bring the hairbrush or the bottle of lotion over to the bed so he could do these things for her, but tonight he just wanted to watch. Finally, he broke the silence between them.

"What are you thinking, Gelsy?"

"You know what I'm thinking, darling." She put down the brush and turned to face him. "I'm thinking of how lonely I'll be if you are locked up at that conference for very long."

She looked so childlike in her pink polka-dotted flannel pajamas, it made his heart beat louder. "How do you think I feel? Just looking at you makes me want to break down and cry sometimes, girl, when I think of going away." He lifted his arms to her. "Come over here."

She walked across the room and knelt on the bed, slowly lowering herself into his embrace. He lifted the covers and pulled her underneath, then ran his hands up and down her body as he put his lips down to hers. For her part, she simply lay tiny and passive, accepting his caresses. This was so unlike her, usually she was a willing partner if not the motivating force in their lovemaking. He pulled back to look at her. "Gelsy, are you OK?"

"Yes, dearest, I'm OK, just tired from the traveling and depressed by Robert's news. It's almost like thinking of you being called up for another tour of duty, isn't it? Although, hopefully not as dangerous. But one never knows these days. Diplomats seem to be targets for terrorists as much as soldiers sometimes. I will worry about you every moment."

"But that's why you gave me this," he said and held out the gold crucifix he'd never taken off since she'd put it around his neck the day of their first sexual encounter. "You asked God to watch over me for you, remember?"

She laughed and put her lips up to the spot where she'd kissed it that day. "Yes, because you were from that moment the dearest person in the world to me, and I couldn't live without you."

"And it helped me when I thought I'd lost you that awful night, Gelsy. I took it out and kissed it, and that's when I could see the vision of you with your parents. That's how I was able to call you back to me."

"Oh, Davey . . . I remember hearing your voice, saying 'You told me not to leave you, how can you leave *me*?' I looked at Mama and Papa, and in their eyes I saw 'Go back and live your life with him. We will be happy for you.'" She pressed the crucifix back against his chest and kissed him gently, then passionately. He slowly began to unbutton her pajama top and feel for her breasts.

"Remember when you told me the French said a woman's breasts should just fit in a champagne glass?" he whispered, sliding down to caress them with his lips.

"Yes. I was afraid you'd want a big-bosomed professional and be disappointed in me," she whispered back, her voice sounding strained.

"And all I saw was the most beautiful, most desirable woman in the world."

He continued worshipping her body with his lips and hands for several minutes, until her breathing told him not to wait any longer. Then he took her gently but with great need. His own body had reached its limit and couldn't wait any longer for her. They merged together until there were no boundaries left, and they were perfectly satisfied to be part of each other's bodies.

Later, still wrapped in the afterglow, they reached out and touched the other's body in wonder.

How can I go back to being without her? The thought ran through his brain, over and over, until it nearly drove him insane. *It will be like when I thought she was dying. I'll be in agony, worrying about her every hour. Is she OK? Is she healthy? Worst of all . . . has she found somebody else?* Because this was his biggest fear. That this beautiful young girl would come to her senses and realize she should be with somebody her own age, better-looking, someone more exciting than a graduate student in biochemistry. She clung to him now because he was a part of her old life. He reminded her of her parents and the Friday "hoots" that had been the focal point of their weeks. In her grief after the accident it was only natural she'd feel safer with an older guy who had her parent's approval. But little girls grow up . . .

"Darling, what's wrong? Why so serious?" She was looking up at him now, wide-eyed.

"Nothing, girl," he replied a little gruffly. "Just can't get this conference thing out of my head."

"I understand. Whenever I was getting ready to leave home for a training session somewhere . . . Paris, Russia, New York . . . I'd always be hit with what I called 'pre-homesick blues.' Mama told me to pretend the trip was already over and I was telling her about how it had gone. The time would fly by so fast, before I knew it that would really be happening. So let's just pretend the conference is all over and we're planning our trip to the Grecian Isles!"

"Your mama was one smart cookie. I'm glad you inherited her bright ideas, girl. Let's do that, start planning the trip now. Give ourselves something to look forward to."

"I thought we could fly to London first, since you've never seen much of Europe. You can probably guess I'd like to see the Royal Ballet at Covent Garden! Then Paris, my birthplace! Then to the south of France, where we catch an ocean liner bound for the Mediterranean. How does that sound?"

"Book the tickets, Gelsy. I'm ready to go." He kissed the top of her head and prayed that nothing would change her eagerness to be with him in the next few months.

CHAPTER 4

"Dr. Yuki Nori called again." Robert was standing in the middle of the lab as David walked through the rear door on his first day back to work. "I'm afraid the news is as grim as I thought. We'll be officially called this afternoon and given a chance to accept or reject, but there will be no time to reconsider. The answer has to be immediate. If we accept, we have to be ready to check into the hotel in Zurich by Thursday, 5:00 p.m., their time. Will you allow me to accept in your name?"

David stood, quietly stunned. It was what he'd been expecting, but was hoping would never come. Even a condemned man facing execution keeps hoping somehow the day will never come.

"Of course, if you're going, I'm going," he replied evenly. "We'll have to hurry, though, if we're going to get the research data in shape by then."

"That's my boy! Poor Gelsy. As if she's not dreading your departure date, even the few days she has left with you will be devoted to churning out material to take with us."

"She'll have to understand what it means to be the wife of a scientist, I'm afraid, Robert. At least it's not like being a doctor's wife. I'm not called out in the middle of the night to deliver babies or anything!"

"And what about her dancing? When will she try to begin again?"

David looked up at the clock. "As of fifteen minutes ago, Robert. She insisted on showing up for the first ballet class this morning."

"She didn't! The little scamp . . . I have half a mind to go over and drag her right out of there. I can't imagine Monsieur is allowing it."

"He said if she promised to just mark the difficult steps for a while and let him be the judge of how much was enough, she could show up. Let's face it, there's no way we could keep her home, Robert."

"You're right, of course. I remember once when she had walking pneumonia and disappeared from her bed. We found her in a jazz workshop, running a 103 degree fever!"

"She's *your* goddaughter, Robert!" David couldn't resist chuckling at this.

"And now she's *your* wife, David."

David felt like a balloon that had suddenly been deflated. It was hard to hear someone refer to Gelsy as his wife. It sounded wrong somehow. It felt like he'd won a prize by accident, didn't deserve it, but loved it too much to give it up.

Luckily, Robert continued, "You realize that day after tomorrow is Christmas, David. I know Gelsy refuses to acknowledge the holidays this year because of her parents, but don't you think we should do something for her? I mean, since we'll be going off and leaving her alone so soon afterward?"

Leaving her alone so soon afterward. That cut like a knife, David thought. Of course Gordie and Mark would take over the classes and would also be there to support her if she needed anything, but her two main supports would both be gone at the same time.

"What *can* we do, Robert? She won't even let me mention anything to do with Christmas."

"Can't take her out to dinner, she wouldn't eat a thing on her plate. Can't get her a present, she'd only get mad at us . . . good question, my boy. You've got two days to consider it," he said, and off he went for another set of test tubes, just as Gordie and Mark entered.

"Behold the blushing groom," shouted Gordie, nearly clearing David off the floor in a bear hug.

"Yeah, *compadre*, you'll have to fill us lesser beings in on all the enlightenments we're missing out on," drawled Mark, settling for a handshake.

"Don't congratulate me so fast. This groom is going to be leaving his bride for an unknown-length of time. Robert wants me to go with him to the WHO conference in Zurich."

This had the effect of a minor earthquake. The two young men took a step back and regarded David with a mixture of awe and pity.

"That conference is going to be a hotbed of controversy, David. You must know that already. Nobody that's going is prepared to give an inch. Seclusion time will be measured in months, if not years!"

"Thank you so much for your vote of confidence, Mark. I really needed that. No, really, what I do need is for you two guys to promise me you'll look out for Gelsy. She's already missing her parents, now she's losing Robert and me at the same time. It's tearing me apart."

Gordie stepped forward to take him by the arms. "David, you already know we'll do everything we can for that girl of yours. After all, we knew and loved her before you did! But tell us, how is she doing, health-wise?"

"Health-wise, she's a miracle. In fact, she's at ballet class right now. Not too shabby for a girl who nearly passed into the Great Beyond about three weeks ago. She said that walking on the sand in Santa Barbara strengthened her leg and helped it heal. Our room at the inn was on the second floor, and she'd barely hold onto my arm when she was climbing the stairs. Said she needed the exercise."

Gordie chortled at this. "That's my *chica*! Ever since she was a little girl, David, she's been impossible to keep down."

Robert walked back in on this, saying, "Well, for land's sakes try to keep her down as much as possible while we're away, you two. Go over to the house and make her cook for you, anything to keep her busy. I'm downright worried about what she'll do if she gets bored."

"Bored? Lonely, I can see, or depressed, Robert. But bored?" David was confused.

"Yes, my boy. All those other things are unlike my goddaughter. Left to her own devices, both of us gone and only the classes Monsieur or Madame allows her to take, I'm afraid she'll get bored. For Gelsy, boredom is the key to danger's door."

"Yeah," Mark chimed in. "Remember the time you and Donald had to go bail her out of jail? Seems she'd gone out break-dancing with a crew of black and Mexican chicks, David. They'd set up a boom box at a mall and were dancing their collective butts off when someone turned them in for obscenity. Gelsy's defense was that she couldn't understand the lyrics and was only dancing to the beat of the music!"

"Right! That was during a semester break when she was supposed to be 'resting,' right?" Gordie had an ear-to-ear grin. "She'd just recovered from pneumonia or something. We ended up dragging her out of a Dance Masters' convention."

Robert let out a groan. "You guys aren't making this any easier for us, you know."

"Sorry. You're right, sir. We will do our best to keep an eye on her while you're away." Mark was immediately remorseful. Gordie just nodded his head.

"I know you will, boys, but you'll also have to take over the intersession classes, and maybe even start off the winter quarter classes, if it comes to that. I'm not taking anything for granted. It's going to be a long haul over at that blasted conference. If there was any way I could get around going, I would. I especially hate taking David with me at a time like this, but rationally, I know it can't be helped. For once I have to admit I can't handle it alone."

"Well, Robert," said David, folding his arms and looking at him calmly. "Isn't that why you suddenly decided you needed a son in your old age? For a backup in times like this?"

"Absolutely correct, my dear boy. I especially needed one I approved of to marry my goddaughter to. Now, let's all get to work and see how much of this material we can get processed in one morning!"

And not too far away, beyond the arched bridge spanning the stream, in the main dance studio a very happy Monsieur was calling out to the class, "And *one*, two three, and *two*, two three . . .," all the while thinking to himself, *No one would believe she is dancing on a leg that was broken less than a month ago. I must not let her do too much today, but how hard it is to stop the dear child! Should I tell her the news, or should I wait, for her health's sake? Madame is right, she will push herself too far. I must be the one to make her modify the steps. Look at her now, she is trying to go into a triple pirouette. If she were to fall, the leg could snap like a twig. But she does it with such ease, it is so hard to make her dummy down the steps. And the chance to dance at the highest level, even for a few weeks, is that so bad? They would make things as easy for her as possible. And Naj is right. We do owe him a favor since he danced at our benefit. Yes, I will tell her the news. She is an adult now. She must make her own decision.*

Chapter 5

Robert and David were late coming home for dinner. They had called Gelsy and told her to eat without them, but when they arrived she had the dinner still waiting for them. The three of them sat down for a meal that was served at the time they should be crawling into bed.

"You two look absolutely beat," Gelsy complained, handing out the bowls.

"We are, my love," Robert groaned scooping up his share of the casserole and sinking down in his chair. "Too tired, really, even to eat."

"Well, try to eat something, anyway. I have some news for you, and it might go down better on a full stomach."

The two men both paused, holding their forks at almost exactly the same angle as if smelling danger. "What kind of news, exactly?" David asked cautiously.

"Well, while you two are gone to Zurich, I have an opportunity to be in New York."

Forks were laid down as both men leaned into the table, waiting for more.

"It seems that Naj heard I recovered from injuries very quickly, and they are still dancing *The Nutcracker* through New Year's Eve. One of their ballerinas just announced she's pregnant and wants to stop dancing *asap*. Can I fill in on her slots as the Snow Queen and the Sugarplum Fairy?"

"Gelsy!" Robert was aghast. "You can't possibly take on a ballerina role so soon!"

"But, Buba, think about it. Both those roles only require real dancing for a very short time. I would be onstage and off again in a matter of minutes, except maybe for a little parading around. And it would keep me occupied while you two are in seclusion."

"I've got no idea what you're talking about, 'Snow Queen' or whatever, but, Gelsy, it does seem like it's just too risky." David couldn't look in her eyes. He stared at the casserole as if it held the answers to his problems, not wanting to say that by "risky" he didn't just mean health risks.

"Oh, Son, you just said exactly the wrong thing," Robert groaned. "Tell her she can't do something, it's too risky—that's like waving a red flag at a bull."

"Buba, I don't mean to be contrary, truly I don't. But this is such an opportunity for me, and it comes at a time when I really need something to take my mind off the loneliness. You want me to stay here in this big, empty house alone? Mama and Papa gone, you two gone? What would I do with myself?"

The two men looked at each other. It did make their objections seem narrow-minded and selfish. She was an adult, after all. Did they trust her to make the right decisions for herself or not?

David finally raised his eyes to hers. "Girl, I want you to be happy more than just about anything in this world. You're right. I never thought of it that way, you being all alone in this house if we were gone. Dancing *The Nutcracker* in New York would be a chance to get away, maybe even get back a little of the holiday spirit you can't bring yourself to face right now."

Robert chimed in, "David is right, I'm being an overprotective godfather, as usual. You know how I can't stand the thought of anything bad happening to you, Gelsy. But if it doesn't go well, I have to trust that you'll know your own limitations and not do anything that would permanently damage your body."

"Thank you both, for letting me grow up and be my own woman for a change," Gelsy laughed. "Now please eat your dinner before it gets cold!"

Getting ready for bed that night, David insisted on rubbing her tired feet with lotion in bed. "How did it feel, girl? Being back in class with Monsieur?"

"Oh, Davey, it felt absolutely divine!" She wiggled her toes and bounced twice on the bed. "I finally felt like my old self again. He didn't want me to put on pointé shoes, but I slipped them on when he wasn't looking, and he didn't notice until class was almost over and I was doing a triple pirouette." She bounced again and giggled. "Then he turned white with fright, but it was too late. I'd already completed it and was on my way! He never said another word after that."

David gently massaged her toes, trying to understand all the ballet lingo but only feeling more and more concerned for her well-being. "But you will monitor yourself, Gelsy? Please promise me that you will know when enough is enough?"

She immediately became serious. "I will, my love. It is my body. I take care of it."

Late as it was, he still needed her. Knowing he had so little time left made him feel empty, and no matter how often he joined with her, he couldn't feel full. This time was a beautiful time, though, and as he slipped into slumber, he heard her whisper, "You see, it is my body. I will take care of it, for you."

Chapter 6

It was time.

Robert and David would leave from the house. They'd already arranged that Gelsy wouldn't accompany them to the airport. "Too much confusion with security and all," Robert said.

And so David found himself saying good-bye to her at the door of Robert's car, feeling as if the heart was being ripped out of his body.

"You will be careful in New York, girl?" was all he could manage.

"You know I will, dearest. And remember, you always have this with you." She touched the spot on his chest where, under the shirt and tie, rested the gold crucifix. "When you find yourself missing me, kiss it. Wherever I am, I'll feel your lips touching mine."

The ride to the airport was mostly silent. Robert tried to engage him in some conversation about the upcoming conference, but David was in another world.

Once at the airport, with all the security checks and hurrying to find their terminal, it finally became clear to him how far away from her he was going. Every gate, every plane landing or departing was just one more reminder that there would be half a world between them. The pain he was feeling only reminded him of the night he'd spent in the hospital chapel, thinking she was on the verge of death and planning his own suicide. "But she didn't die, and the two of you were married in that same chapel just a few weeks later," he kept trying to tell himself. But the pain didn't let up.

Eventually their plane boarded. It was a long flight; no amount of food or in-flight movies could relieve the boredom of a flight that long. When they arrived, they immediately took a taxi to their hotel. The problem with that was once they checked into the hotel, they were automatically checked into conference security, and David didn't realize it until it was too late. He'd called her from the airport and left a message that they'd arrived safely, but was looking forward to having a long conversation with her after arriving. That would be impossible now. He cursed his stupidity.

Robert was in the next room, but they were to check with conference security before even visiting between rooms. David turned on the television. Obviously, it had been tuned in to only a few select channels—old movies, entertainment television, news, and sports. David didn't care much for sports and wasn't overly interested in most old movies, but he was surprised to notice on the entertainment news a flash that Gelsy Grandwood, the young ballerina who had been through a horrific car accident that took both her parents' lives only a month ago, would be dancing *The Nutcracker* in New York starting tomorrow night. Her partner would be Naj Nadinsky, the dancer who had partnered her in the *Romeo and Juliet* pas de deux the night of the accident. Strange, Gelsy hadn't mentioned Naj would be her partner, but he should have guessed.

When David finally got clearance to visit Robert's room, the first thing he wanted to know was "Did you know Naj would be her partner?"

Robert was stunned. "No, my boy, I had no idea. But I guess I should have known. He has his choice of ballerinas, and it's only natural he'd pick her. What am I thinking? He's the reason she got invited in the first place! All this talk about showing young dancers how it's possible to recover from an injury and continue dancing, pregnant ballerinas wanting a vacation, heck! He just wanted her back in New York."

"Back in New York, and I'm locked up in Zurich. I'll bet he's having a good laugh about that, Robert."

"The first thing you've got to do is take it easy. David. Gelsy loves you, and if you can't trust her by now, then you'll be having problems the entire time of your marriage. Not to mention it will take your mind completely off the business at hand here."

"I know, I know," David groaned. "I've got to remember that I was a scientist before I was a husband! But it's so hard, Robert. Like having a major surgery without anesthesia."

"My poor boy. I remember the feeling so well." Robert was sitting next to him with his arm around his shoulders. "Believe it or not, I went through exactly the same pain when Donald and Adele took off on their honeymoon. Yes, we'd decided that it was the best thing to do, that they marry so she could stay in this country. But when the deed was done and they were gone, I felt like a fish being filleted. Lord, how I loved that woman! And I see her whenever I look at her daughter. She is truly her mother's child, David, which is why you must let her go her own way sometimes. It's the only thing to do if you want to keep her, in the long run."

"I keep forgetting how much you loved Adele, or that Gelsy might even be your child, Robert. How can you live with not knowing that for sure?"

"Because she'll always be Donald's daughter and my goddaughter no matter whose natural child she is. As I said, the important thing to remember is that she is Adele, through and through!"

Later that night, while trying to sleep alone in the hard hotel bed, David tried to imagine how it must have been for Robert, meeting Gelsy's mother at the same time as his best friend and both of them falling in love with her. Gelsy herself wasn't surprised to discover they'd had a *ménage de trios* for many years, but David couldn't get over the idea of loving a woman and sharing her with another man. For them it was a family unit, though, and had been a happy one all the years leading up the car accident. Robert could barely hang onto life himself after that; he only hung on for Gelsy's sake. That she might actually be his biological child wasn't as important to him as the fact she was Adele's daughter.

What message could he send out to her? What would be intimate enough and yet appropriate enough for strangers to read and attempt to decode? He was a scientist and no good with words. Then he remembered the note he had left for her the first time he'd had to leave her sleeping, "Hate to leave, will see you soon." He looked at the seven words and decided he could do no better.

The next day brought a news flash on the entertainment channel that eclipsed Gelsy's joining *The Nutcracker* cast. A visiting ballet company from South America, security guards firmly in place, had been forced to leave the country minus one dancer. In spite of every precaution, their lead male danseur, Felipe Rodriquez, had flown the coop and was now reportedly rehearsing somewhere in New York. Word on the street was that he'd been offered a role in the last few performances of *The Nutcracker*, since it was the one ballet whose choreography was fairly standard. He could step in and compliment Naj as the Snow King when the former was dancing the Cavalier, and vice-versa.

The competition between the two—one so dark and the other so blond, each with an entirely different style—would be a treat for every balletomane in the city. Even those who had already seen the ballet would rush out and buy tickets to one of the last remaining shows, especially when it was announced they would be trading off partnering Gelsy Grandwood!

The WHO conference was as heavy and strained as David had imagined. He felt danger at every session that every word he spoke was being measured for hidden meanings. Robert was right; it took every ounce of his concentration to maintain a clear head. Meals were eaten in hushed conversation, which didn't help digestion. When he finally returned to his room at night he felt haggard and old beyond his years.

And in his room there was only the one channel to watch. Every night it seemed to have a new lead story on the "Big Ballet Brouhaha," as the reporters had named it. A love triangle between Gelsy, Naj, and . . . Felipe.

David's name never appeared, except as "the husband." He was dismissed as being "an older man," "the scientist, who unwisely left a young bride alone immediately following the wedding."

She was, of course, "only eighteen," and had married in haste, before she had even left the hospital, following her parents' deaths. He had taken advantage of her state of mind. Felipe had used this as an excuse to justify his attentions to a married woman to his own parents! Given a humanitarian leave for visiting his father, dying of cancer, he was shown going to Mass with his strictly Catholic mother and sisters, head held high. Friends of the family were assured he would have no trouble convincing Gelsy to obtain an annulment of her ill-advised marriage from the Church. She had been too young and under too much stress to make a valid decision at the time.

Everything David had feared, and then there was more.

When Felipe returned to New York, reporters were watching his every move, and it wasn't long before they discovered his moves in the evening that took him to Gelsy's hotel, where he had just recently checked in.

By this time Naj was ready to strangle the Latin Lothario. Hadn't he brought Gelsy to New York for his benefit alone? But Gelsy, as sweet and compliant in her partnering as always, still seemed to slip away from him when the dancing was finished and the curtain came down.

It was just at this time Robert came in the room to find David listening to the latest ballet news flash while sipping his third Scotch on the rocks.

"My boy, why are you watching this claptrap? Don't you see why they're allowing you to see it? It's a ploy to distract you from the conference. Why else would you be getting this channel and no one else?"

"I didn't realize that, Robert. So I'm the only one here privileged to watch the day-by-day account of my wife cheating on me with some South American Casanova?"

"Don't make me knock that glass out of your hand and create a really dramatic scene here, David. We might, just might, be being taped, you know. This is my godchild we're talking about, and I will not hear you talk about her like that. I won't believe she is being unfaithful to you in any way until she tells me so, herself."

"Hang around a few minutes, Robert. They'll show the security camera footage where Felipe's going up to her room, knocking on her door, and being admitted. Then the dinner cart arrives, and he doesn't come out again for four or five hours. What would you have me believe?"

"That they're talking. I don't know . . . but I can't believe this of my Gelsy. It goes against everything she believes in."

"Well, her mother managed two lovers. Maybe Gelsy thinks she shouldn't be stuck with just one."

This time the shot glass did go flying across the room, like it had been fired from a gun. David felt as though he'd been slapped hard across the face, and from the look on Robert's face, there was no mistaking his intent.

"Don't you ever speak of Gelsy's mother, or Gelsy, like that to me again."

Robert turned and left the room.

Chapter 7

Gelsy was so very tired.

Seeing the line of autograph-hunters in front of the stage door a full hour before the matinee didn't help. "Oh. Miss Grandwood," "Over here, Miss Gelsy," on and on until the little ache in her head threatened to multiply tenfold.

Why did no one think to call her "Mrs. Chaveral"?

By the time she got into the rehearsal area, the little headache had taken root and begun to blossom. She wanted to bum some heavy-duty aspirin off a stagehand and get them down in the privacy of her dressing room, but there was no more time. She simply had to hurry and dress down, but as what? She'd forgotten, was she Snow Queen or Fairy tonight? Better check the call-board. Snow Queen, all in white and silver, then. *Like a bride*, she thought, wondering what she'd wear if she and Davey were to be married again in a church.

Oh, how silly. I'll wear my mother's wedding gown, of course. She smiled at the thought. Davey liked her dressed as Juliet, and her mother's gown was very much in that style. Her parents had both loved the Franco Zeffirelli version of *Romeo and Juliet* that had come out a few years previously, so they'd given their entire wedding a medieval theme.

"*Buenos Dios*, Gelsy." It was the new dancer, the South American boy who had been so thrilled to find out she spoke Spanish. True, her Mexican dialect differed from his, but they could make themselves understood easy enough. What was his name? Felipe. And today he'd partner her for the first time. In rehearsal they'd worked well together. Felipe handled her so much like Rennie. Gelsy could close her eyes and believe her old partner was back, but there was an extra-gentle touch from this boy. He never overstepped the boundaries and always kept his hands and other body parts to himself when not directly necessary for the lifts and supports. Gelsy appreciated his consideration. She was tired of dodging Naj's advances, which had become a daily nuisance.

"How's the hot love affair going?" Gelsy shared her dressing room with another ballerina in the cast, named Ranielle. "I mean, Gelsy, now you'll have the reporters crawling out of the woodwork wanting to know if you think this new guy is better than Naj!"

"Oh, thanks, Ranni, I really needed to hear *that*!" Gelsy shot back. "Here I am trying to dig up some aspirin already, and you hit me with even more delightful news."

Ranni was diving headfirst into her dance bag. "You want aspirin, codeine, or anything stronger . . . I got it."

"Thanks, the aspirin will be fine."

"Here you go." The petite redhead popped two tablets in Gelsy's hand.

"Much obliged, I'm sure." Gelsy immediately gulped them down, not minding a bit that they looked like they'd spent rather a long time in the bottom of Rennie's dance bag.

"Poor girl, I should have such problems! Why is it nobody thinks for a minute the two best-looking men in the ballet world might be interested in *me*?"

"Might be the husband and two kids, Rennie. Good Lord, girl! Why are you even still dancing?"

"To help support a husband and two kids. My husband is an artist, sweetie. No insurance."

"Right. Hopefully my husband will always work in a research lab with good pay and great insurance benefits."

"From your mouth to God's ears, sweetie!"

*****

The television was replaying a film clip of Gelsy and Felipe dancing together for the first time, as the King and Queen of Snow. *Yeah, bet he was doing a real snow job on her, too*, David reflected drunkenly. He hadn't been this close to being dead drunk in a long time. Not since Randy . . . *Don't go there now*, he told himself. *That's all you need.*

Well, why not? He'd let himself get attached to Randy, and Randy went out and got himself blown up. Then he went and got himself attached to Gelsy, and he knew from day one it was a damned stupid thing to do. Every minute of happiness he had with her would be repaid by hours of agony and suffering in the future. This was just the beginning.

He forced himself to watch the clip. No doubt about it—they were amazing together. Felipe was a dead ringer for Rennie, only older and more polished. He handled Gelsy with an aura of adoration that would melt the hardest heart. They made magic together.

David had to laugh to think of how all this was sitting with Naj. The Russian had brought Gelsy to New York to be *his* Christmas present, not to have some Latin lover come steal her away. No wonder it was the love triangle of the ballet world right now. Naj was dancing better than ever, as if to overshadow Gelsy's and Felipe's growing popularity. And he hadn't given up on getting Gelsy for himself either. Television cameras followed him as he tried to follow her daily, offering her his chauffeur-driven town car for shopping trips and having the company manager talk her into late-night suppers, supposed to iron out contract details, which would evaporate into tête-à-têtes when Naj arrived and the manager mysteriously disappeared. It was all so romantic. Which lover would she choose?

CHAPTER 8

David was essentially locked in his room, like a naughty boy on a time-out. He'd woken up that morning to a terrific hangover, but he took a cold shower, dressed, and somehow made it to the correct conference room where he was to deliver his most important individual speech of the session. This was the bedrock of all the research begun at Carmichael and given breadth and scope at UCSM under Robert. How did he do? He had no damned idea.

He was back in his room, an untouched lunch tray in front of him and a stomach that churned whenever he looked at it.

Robert hadn't come near him since the night before, when he'd sent the shot glass flying. Now when David tried to go next door, he was met by a burly security guard in the hall and told he wasn't on Robert's guest list! In fact, he was told he was restricted to his room until further information was received. Meals would be delivered to him.

The next day would be New Year's Eve. *Great way to celebrate the New Year*, David thought ironically. *Wonder how Gelsy will be celebrating . . . or who will she be celebrating it with?*

He'd promised himself he wasn't going to turn on the TV again, but promises were made to be broken. He sat through an hour of dreary stories about Hollywood personalities (he couldn't bring himself to say "stars") until finally he saw what he'd been waiting for, a sign in the background that said, "Coming up next—Ballet Brouhaha!"

Sitting through the six commercial spots almost drove David insane. When the show finally did reappear, an impossibly chirpy blonde personality sat in front of a screen that flashed images of Gelsy dancing, first with Felipe and then with Naj. "The ballet world is reeling over the news of a backstage brawl between Felipe Rodriquez and Naj Nadinsky last night, following the evening performance of *Nutcracker*. Both men had accidentally been scheduled to dance with ballerina Gelsy Grandwood, and in the final moments before the show Naj pulled rank and forced Gelsy to change costume and dance with him. He should have realized that Felipe's Latin blood would never allow such a slight to his manhood to go unpunished. The curtain had barely come down when the *mucho* macho Felipe threw himself on Naj and had to be pulled off by stagehands."

After yet another commercial break the story continued. Naj got his comeuppance later that evening. When he tried to visit Gelsy at the hotel to apologize, he was turned away, while Felipe breezed past him with a grin. *He*, after all, was also a guest there! And that wasn't all. Once again the security camera footage showed dinner for two being delivered to Gelsy's room, and not five minutes later, Felipe was knocking at her door. "Well, that about cinches the deal," David muttered to himself, pouring out the last of the Scotch.

There was a knock at the door, but he didn't even bother to answer. After a second knock, he just shouted, "Who is it?"

The answer came back, "It's your dad. May I speak to you?"

David had to chuckle at this, but he got up and unlocked the door so Robert could come in.

"What's up, Robert?"

"Start packing, my boy. You'll be flying out of here in the morning."

"No way! I'm not leaving you here by yourself."

"Yes, you are, because the conference is over—although no one knows it yet. Your talk today put the final wheels in motion, and for that I have to thank you, David. I know what it cost you to get up there and deliver, what with everything that's been riding on your back the past few days. But you came through, Son! Tomorrow a news conference will be called, and all I'll have to do is answer questions on what our part in the proceedings was and how I feel about the outcome. That much I can do on my own. Meanwhile, the ambassador is flying to New York in the morning and just happens to have an empty seat on the embassy plane. You're scheduled to be on it. You'll spend New Year's Eve with Gelsy and hopefully get this whole mess straightened out one way or another. Understand?"

"Understand? I'm flabbergasted. Are you sure, Robert? You're not just saying this to get rid of me, are you?"

"No, David. I wouldn't lie to you. It's all true. Give Gelsy my love and tell her I'll meet her at home the day after New Year. Hopefully she'll be finished with New York by then."

"Robert . . . what am I going to do if I get there and find it's all true?"

"I don't believe it for a minute, but if it is, I suppose you'll go on living, Son."

*****

The ambassador's plane made good time. *That's the advantage to having your own security checks and takeoff times*, David thought. It would be nice to always fly at the government's expense.

From all the news reports he knew he'd arrived on the last day Gelsy would be dancing, New Year's Eve, and once again it was going to be a fight to the finish. She had requested her last performance be a matinee, and both men had demanded to be scheduled to partner her. As of curtain time no one knew which would be the winner.

David went directly to the hotel and demanded the key to her room. As her husband, they had to give it to him, although there was much consternation as he marched to the elevator and went up to the fifth floor. At that time of the day, no one was around to pay attention— over at Lincoln Center the matinee performance was just beginning. David immediately turned on the entertainment channel, ordered a bottle of Scotch, and settled himself in. Finally he got the news he'd been looking for at almost the same time the liquor arrived: Gelsy would be dancing with Naj. The Russian had pulled rank again. Any pleasure David might have felt in this was doused by a quick interview with Felipe outside the stage door, where he announced in his best bravado voice and broken English that the "Russian has her for matinee, I see her tonight."

David looked at the clock. Matinee performance, change clothes, get back to hotel, at least two to three more hours. He put his head back on the sofa.

He awoke with the shock of not remembering where he was, but then he saw her walk through the door. She was alone, and at first seemed terrified a man was in her room. When she realized it was David, she started to run to him.

"Oh, Davey . . ." Something in the way he stood and looked at her made her stop. He was still holding the shot glass in one hand he'd held patiently balanced on his knee all this time. Now he downed the last of the Scotch in it before putting the glass on the coffee table.

"Surprised to see me, Gelsy?" he said, every word heavy with meaning.

"I don't know what . . ." There was a knock at the door.

"Expecting someone, Gelsy?"

"It's probably the dinner cart," she said, and went to sign for it. The linen-covered cart with place settings for two and a red rose in a bud vase was wheeled in.

"Settings for two? You surely weren't expecting me, were you, girl?" David knew his voice was getting angry, but he couldn't stop himself now. Everything was playing out exactly as he'd seen it in his dreams, No, in his worst nightmares. Now all that was needed was the other knock on the door. Oh, there it was!

By this time Gelsy was simply standing in the middle of the room, staring at him as if she'd never seen him before. The knock was repeated. "Better get that, girl," David hissed, as he poured himself another drink.

Gelsy turned and walked to the door and opened it, and Felipe swaggered in.

"Well done, Gel-zee. Buena! Naj *es* . . . how you say, furious!" Then he realized there was another man in the room. "But Gel-zee, you no introduce me to your amigo."

"Not amigo, *espouso*, Felipe. This is my husband, David Chaveral."

"Oh, no . . . he is too soon! We are not ready, Gel-zee!"

"What do you mean, 'not ready,' Felipe? You don't have your bags packed yet for a quick elopement to some foreign country?" David snarled.

Felipe was looking in confusion from one to the other and merely repeating, "Not ready . . ."

"He doesn't understand half of that, David. He only understands that we were planning to work out a suitable escape plan this evening, and here comes our accomplice now." With a flourish she indicated another man who had mysteriously appeared behind David's left shoulder as all this was taking place. "David, meet Antonio, Felipe's 'significant other.' My bedroom has an adjoining door to a suite on the other side of the hallway and that's where we'll be going now, so please pick up your suitcase and bottle and follow me." She began walking briskly through the suite without even looking at David.

Antonio obligingly jumped forward to take the single suitcase. "You just get the glass and bottle, David. I've got Gelsy's dinner ready for her over there. Sorry, I didn't know you were coming. I would have ordered for two!"

David followed in a haze. The suite on the other side was almost identical, and a smaller, less formal version of the dinner was laid out on the table. David walked over to the sofa and placed his bottle and glass on the coffee table as it was next door as she sat down to eat. "Care to tell me what's going on, Gelsy?" he stammered.

"There's not much to tell. Where Felipe comes from, it's a crime to be homosexual. That's the real reason he defected. He and Antonio wanted to be together freely. Everyone was so focused on Felipe, they never noticed that a baggage handler for the ballet company had gone missing at the same time. And if they did, they wouldn't want it advertised." She unwrapped a cold turkey submarine sandwich. "Would you like half of this? You look like you need real food."

David mindlessly sat down at the table and started to eat. "So you took Antonio in and faked a romance with Felipe so the two of them could be together?"

"Just until the season was over. I thought you were in seclusion in Zurich, and by the time you heard all the rumors I'd have had a chance to explain. And the three of us were plotting a way for me to leave the company because of too much drama between Felipe and Naj, so I could return to my husband . . . my first and only real love."

"And the late-night hookups with Felipe?"

"Teaching him English. My mother spent much of her life teaching English as a second language. I had Gordie go over to the house and send me some of her tapes. Luckily, Antonio's mother was an American, and he grew up speaking English."

"And Naj?"

"Knows nothing of this. He's terribly homophobic, like a lot of straight male dancers are because they get hit on so much. This way we were able to keep Felipe's family from knowing too. It was hard enough on them to lose him when he defected. But Felipe and Antonio both know that eventually the truth has to come out, just for their own sanity. They can't live a lie forever."

David had eaten the sandwich half and a few of the fries. The booze in his system was being diluted by the food and the water—things were looking a little clearer.

"So let me get this straight. I was completely wrong, and Robert was completely right."

"If by that you mean that Buba never for a minute believed I was unfaithful to you, and you thought I was sleeping with Felipe, then the answer is yes." Her voice was as cold as the frosty New York air outside Times Square as it readied for the big countdown into the New Year.

"Gelsy, I'm . . ."

"Just don't say anything right now, David. I'm too tired to deal with it." She got up, kicked off her boots, and stretched across the bed, fully-clothed.

David returned to the sofa and his bottle of Scotch and poured himself a shot, but somehow he couldn't get it to his lips no matter how hard he tried. All he saw was that tiny body dressed in a wool pantsuit lying exhausted, prone on the bed, and his heart began to break. He sat the glass down on the table with a *thud* so loud, Gelsy looked up and saw his shoulders shaking. In a minute she was sitting on the sofa next to him, and he was sobbing in her arms like a child.

"Don't tell me you've stopped loving me because I'm such an idiot, girl!" was all he could say.

"You're not an idiot, Davey. I was playing a dangerous game, just counting on the fact you were in seclusion and wouldn't know what I was up to. Your messages were so cryptic I couldn't tell if you knew or not, and I just kept thinking it was all for a good cause. The last performances of the ballet made more money that all the others, just because of a few crazy rumors! But that meant a lot of dancers don't have to worry about getting rehired next season, you know."

"Robert knew there had to be something else going on. I'm supposed to be a scientist, but I took those crazy rumors for facts and came back here to catch you with your lover. Damn! How could I have been so stupid?"

"You weren't being stupid." She took his head in her hands and kissed away the tears, laughing. "You were being a man in love. How can I fault you for that? If you'd loved me less, would you have come tearing across the Atlantic to face down the challenger? Oh, my darling, I do love you so very much!"

Now she kissed him on the mouth, tasting the Scotch he'd been using to kill the pain. Slipping out of her jacket, she put his hands on her breasts under the silk blouse. The sofa was large and comfortable; she saw no reason to move from there. Only to unbutton her blouse and his shirt, then remove other items of clothing while still managing to stay connected at the lips.

Finally they were both nude and feeling their way around the sofa, finding the ideal spot to settle into. They settled just in time; he was attempting to press himself into her with a ferocity that she'd never seen in him before. It was as if he had to be connected with her to really believe she was his—that they were together again. Finally, they were settled and together, and the hairs on the back of his neck stood up as the thought passed through his mind, *Man and wife!*

For a long time they lay on the sofa. When she began to shiver from the draft blowing across the room, he covered her with items of discarded clothing and his own body but refused to let her leave. She was in his arms again, and he couldn't let go of her just yet; it still hurt too much. Every breath he took was bringing him a little closer to realizing what a fool he'd been to create a world of suspicion and doubt where there was only trust and love on her part.

"Gelsy, I can't say I'll never be afraid again. I just love you too much, and I don't know if I'll ever feel like I deserve to have you all to myself. But promise me, if you ever have any thoughts like that, you'll at least be honest and tell me right away. I could stand that easier than thinking you were keeping a secret from me."

"I will promise anything you ask, Davey, anything that will ease your mind. But can you believe me if I say I cannot imagine ever loving a man the way I love you?"

He lay perfectly still, trying to digest that thought. Imaging that he was really the only man in the world she wanted, in her bed, in her life . . .

"I have this feeling that I want to do something . . . I'm not sure how to say it exactly, girl. I feel like, even when I took the wedding vows, there was some kind of holding back. Not that I didn't want to give myself to you, just that I couldn't. Do you understand any of this?"

"I think so. You were afraid to give yourself completely because you thought it was only a matter of time before I'd find someone else, somebody better than you in some way for me. Is that right?"

"That's exactly right."

"But . . . there is nobody in the world better than you for me, in any way. Can you accept that?"

"I've never been able to accept that. I don't know if I can now. I'll just figure you haven't met him yet."

"Then we'll never be truly happy together, Davey. You'll only be loving me but waiting for me to leave you. What kind of marriage would that be?"

"That's what I mean, Gelsy. If I can give myself completely to you, then I won't care. Whatever you do that makes you happy will be OK. If you find somebody else, I'll just turn around and walk away, wishing you both well."

"I don't want to talk about this anymore tonight, Davey. I'm cold, and I want to take a hot shower and get into bed. Please, can I do that?"

"Of course you can, girl . . ." He released her from a grip of iron and watched her walk into the bathroom without a backward look. He heard the shower run, then saw her walk out with a towel wrapped around her, and immediately he was transported back to the first night they spent together in her room, when she walked in from the guest bathroom clad only in a towel. He told her then he'd wanted to try something, something he'd never wanted to try on the prostitutes who had been his only sexual partners up until that day. Now, before she put on her pajamas . . .

What was he thinking? Lying naked on the couch in the middle of a pile of clothes, reeking of sweat, booze, and sex. He slipped into his jockey shorts and began to gather up the articles of clothing, piling hers on one chair and his on another. Then he went into the bathroom and took a quick shower himself.

By the time he got back, she'd hung up her clothing and put on her pink pajamas, the ones that made her look like a little girl. All he had was his jockey shorts. His pajamas were in his suitcase, but it hadn't been opened yet, and he saw no reason to bother now. He'd sleep in his shorts.

"There's no reason for me to go out the door in the other suite tomorrow, unless you want to go out with me," Gelsy said. "Someone downstairs must have told the reporters you'd checked in. It was probably in all the news flashes last night. Felipe usually leaves there about midnight and goes to his own room. Then Antonia sleeps there the rest of the night.

"We can switch with Antonio in the morning and check out together. If anybody asks anything, we'll just say you don't know what the big deal was. Felipe came over for his English lesson as usual, and I helped out.

"That should wrap things up nicely and have them screaming in frustration." Gelsy smiled sweetly. "And there's nothing I love more than a frustrated gossipmonger!"

David crawled under the covers, looking mischievous. "Or, I could walk out of here with you thrown over my shoulder, bound and gagged. Take your choice!" And he began unbuttoning the pajama top.

He had taken her too quickly before. Seeing her walk out wrapped in only the towel reminded him of other ways he could please and excite her . . . ways that excited him as well. Kissing her sweet breasts that always reminded him of little French pastries, he worked his way downward to the tiny, gentle creature that made its home between her thighs. He stroked the soft fur and kissed its pink lips. She began to shudder in earnest now, and for the first time she begged him to stop and simply take her. Their time apart had been too much for her too.

When it was over they both lay wrapped up in each other's arms, completely exhausted. For some reason David remembered the evening he'd crawled into her hospital bed and they'd tried to make love in whatever way they could at that point. When it was over, he was hit by the realization that she was really going to live. That thought made him capable of giving up the ghost of his army buddy, Randy, who had died in his arms after a bomb blast. Now if he felt he could accept the fact she loved him, maybe he could let go of the fear of losing her too. Maybe . . .

They fell into unconsciousness, intertwined, only to be awakened an hour later by the screams of the crowds outside their windows. The ball was starting to fall in Times Square to mark the New Year. They could see fireworks even through the closed blinds, so they just lay as they were and whispered "Happy New Year" to each other, aware it was the first time they'd seen a new year in together.

"Girl!" David's voice came from somewhere deep inside him. "Girl, I mean, Gelsy, I have a feeling like God is telling me it's time."

"Darling, time for what?" She tried to force herself awake, but it was hard. It was so delicious, lying there, almost completely under the covers, feeling so warm and naked next to him.

"For me to let go."

"Then come to me, my darling. Send yourself to me the same way you did that night in the chapel. When I was with my parents, and we were on our way to heaven, I saw you then, Davey. Don't you realize? You gave yourself to me that night, when you were ready to die to be with me."

"Then why this, Gelsy? Why this terrible fight I'm having with jealousy? Why all the fears that you'll grow up and want somebody new?"

"It's not giving yourself to me, my love. You just have never felt I gave myself wholly to you. Or that if I thought I did, I was just too immature to know my own mind."

"Yeah, that's it! I know how I feel, and God knows how I feel about you. But I guess you're right. I've never completely accepted that you loved me the same way."

She curled up a little closer and kissed his shoulder. "You know, I've always been especially fond of your shoulders? Ever since that day you took Rennie down and told him to leave me alone. I could see the muscles tighten in your shoulders when you reached out to grab him and push me away. My knight in shining armor!"

"You see, you're a little girl in love with a fairy tale, Gelsy."

"*Non*, my dearest. After we'd made love that day and you tried to leave me, I had to stop the car because you were calling my name. You could say nothing, only hold onto the car window and shake. That is why I put the crucifix around your neck, to give you something to steady your nerves. You were no knight in a fairy tale then, darling, just a man, frightened and lonely."

"It was like feeling withdrawal from heroin again. I realized you'd sucked the soul right out of me, and even walking back to the dorm alone was too much to take. I couldn't have made it, or through that night in the hospital chapel, without the crucifix, Gelsy."

"So you see, I did give myself to you completely. My soul was contained in that cross of gold around your neck, Davey. As long as you wear it, you carry my soul with you."

Chapter 9

They woke up in the morning to a breakfast cart being delivered to their door with a little note attached: "Compliments of Antonio and friend." Sitting with the curtains open to look out on the balcony, they agreed it was the best breakfast they'd ever eaten.

Checkout time was 11:00 a.m. and it was already 9:30 a.m. The big breakfast had made them both sleepy, so Gelsy called down and gave a late checkout time of 3:00 p.m. Then they crawled back into bed and were asleep in spoon position before a minute had fully passed.

It took over an hour for the breakfast stupor to wear off, but when it did, they found themselves curled lazily around each other in a way that could only lead to one thing. David took it very slowly, reassuring himself at every step that this was his *wife* he was making love to, not some teenaged girl who might dump him the minute somebody better-looking walked over the horizon.

They shared a shower and got dressed while watching the latest news broadcasts. The World Health conference was ending, and they could see footage of Robert addressing the delegates although they couldn't hear what he was saying. That would have to wait until they were all at home together.

Lunch was on a plane headed for Los Angeles, and they were home in plenty of time to fix a home-cooked dinner. A message from Robert said he'd be flying in very late, not to wait up. They left a note that they'd plan a late breakfast to share with him. The next day was Sunday, and they could all go to Mass together, then for lunch afterward.

Snuggling under the covers Gelsy murmured, "It is *so good* to be back in my own bed."

Sitting on the edge of the bed in his pajamas, David played with her hair and laughed, "Isn't it *our* bed now, girl?"

"Oh, yes, it is! That was so thoughtless of me, Davey." She sat straight up to throw her arms around his shoulders.

"It's OK, Gelsy. I get the picture. We're in this together, right?"

"Absolutely right, my darling!" And she kissed him in a way that couldn't be misunderstood.

*****

David came down for breakfast after waking up to an empty bed and the unmistakable smell of waffles. Robert stood in the entryway, ready to give him a hug, a handshake, and enough exclamations of joy at seeing him, indicating that he knew all was forgiven. They both turned to go into the breakfast Gelsy had prepared for them. Everything was ready—bacon, waffles, biscuits, syrup . . . but what were the little sticks mounted in balls of biscuit dough and standing like toy soldiers, their blue heads facing outward, around both men's plates?

Gelsy had a strangely mischievous tone to her voice as she announced, "Gentlemen, be seated."

"Of course, dear girl," Robert said, easing into his chair, "but what am I to do with the little sticks?"

"Whatever you like, Buba. Helping us start by picking out names would be a good start."

There was a moment of recognition, and Robert flew up out of his chair. "Gelsy, you're *pregnant*?!"

"Yes, Buba. And now you must take care of me like you took care of Mama when she was carrying me."

David sat stupefied, staring at the little sticks in awe.

"We're . . . going to have a baby?" He was suddenly so frightened he wanted to run away. A father? How could he be a father?! He had just proven what a lousy husband he was. When the slightest hint of scandal came up, he was ready to believe his wife was being unfaithful to him.

Gelsy was, as usual, one step ahead of him. She walked around the table and settled herself in his lap. "Yes, my darling Davey. We are going to have a baby. This big empty house needs more life in it, and by the time the baby comes, you will have your degree. You will be the best father any child ever had, dearest, and Buba will be the best grandfather."

Robert nearly floated off the floor. "Oh, my darling girl, I feel like I've been waiting my whole life for this moment! How wretched that your Mama and Papa can't be here. But I have to believe they are in heaven, inspecting all the baby angels and picking out the perfect one for you." He picked Gelsy up off David's lap and twirled her around the room.

"Hey, be careful there with my wife!" David jumped up and snatched her from Robert's overeager embrace. "She has to take it easy!"

"Dear, I'll be taking my ballet classes and doing everything as usual. I can't be a baby myself. There should be no problem as long as I am careful."

David looked down into her laughing eyes and felt himself unwrapping years of isolation. She was carrying his baby, right now, right this minute! He was holding not just her, but the two of them. There was a baby inside her that needed a father . . .

Robert put a firm hand on his shoulder and guided him back to his chair.

"Gelsy, I've seen that look on his face before. The night of the accident when Gordie went to fetch him from the chapel, he came in and saw me break down, and he thought it meant you were gone. I told him you were alive, and he got that same look on his face. Like it was just too much for him to take in."

"But it's happy news. And I insist you both force yourself to eat some of the breakfast I have cooked for you," Gelsy scolded, "so we can make it to 11:00 a.m. Mass! Then we are going shopping and just look . . . look, mind you . . . at baby things so we can decide how to fix up the nursery. I've decided Mama and Papa's old room will do for that because it means their spirits can watch over the baby."

"Wonderful idea, sweetheart. Now David, remember how to lift your fork to your mouth with food in it, like this . . ." And Robert made a great show of demonstrating. "You must remember that you're going to have to teach a kid to eat, old man, so better start practicing yourself. I'll warn you, once a baby comes you may not find enough time to eat yourself!"

"At least he has a while to prepare, Buba. I am only just now expecting. The test can measure after forty-eight hours, so he has over eight months to get used to the idea."

Robert paused with his fork halfway to his mouth. "You mean . . . you're only two days along?!"

"Yes. I stopped taking the pills when you and Davey went to Zurich so they would be out of my system when he came home to me. And it worked, like magic!" Gelsy laughed like a little girl who had just pulled a great joke on her elders.

"But my dear, you shouldn't be announcing it to anyone else for a while, you know. Not until the first trimester is over, at least . . . especially for a first baby."

David looked alarmed. "Why is that, Robert?"

"Well . . ." Robert paused, obviously unhappy he brought up the subject. "A first baby can sometimes be very delicate, and it's easy to have a miscarriage."

"Oh, Buba, don't go making Davey afraid for me! I am very healthy. Didn't I just dance *The Nutcracker* after recovering from a car accident? I am young and strong, like my mother was."

At the mention of Adele, Robert's face took on a younger, softer look. "Your mother. My dear, I can remember the night she announced that she was expecting *you*. We were all so very happy." He put his head down for a moment, and Gelsy walked around the table to press his head against her abdomen.

"If it is a boy, it will be Robert. If it is a girl, Roberta," she said quietly.

*****

Kneeling at Mass, David tried to make himself believe he was going to be a father. It had all happened so quickly. Gelsy was lonely for her parents, and having a child would help fill the void—he could understand that. But was she really ready, at eighteen, to be a mother? Were they ready to be parents, married only a few months?!

He bowed his head and tried desperately to make contact with God. *Tell me it's right, that it's all for the best*, he asked. *Tell me I'm ready to be a father.*

CHAPTER 10

January, February, March, and it was almost time for Gelsy's birthday. Her joke was that she wanted maternity clothes for birthday presents because she was finally starting to show a teensy, tiny bit. She certainly didn't try to hide it. If anything, she went out of her way to wear skintight tops that accentuated her growing baby bump.

David had been offered an entry-level teaching position for the spring quarter, when he would finally have his doctorate. His oral exams were set almost to coincide with Gelsy's birthday, and she said it would be her other birthday present.

Mark and Gordie were being especially helpful that Saturday, getting the data together he'd need for his orals. The lab was teeming with last-minute notations before taking the equipment down when the phone rang.

"Yes, he's here. David, it's Student Health. Gelsy was just brought in from dance class!"

A shadow fell over everything. It was as if something expected but dreaded had happened. David grabbed the phone and said, "Yes, yes, yes . . . I'll be right there." Hanging up, he looked at them and said simply, "I have to go."

They brought him in to see her as soon as he arrived, but it was already too late, the baby was lost. She'd fallen in class. It was just one of those things that happens. She was OK otherwise; she'd be able to have other babies. Just not this one.

And she wouldn't look at him. No matter what he said, she didn't seem to hear it. It was the same when Robert arrived. She was deaf and mute to the world. Her baby was dead, and it was all her own fault. She'd never forgive herself.

"What are we going to do, Robert?" David was a wreck, nearly as bad as he'd been the night of the accident. It was his baby, too, and he mourned it. But more than anything, he worried about his wife.

"This was my worst fear, and it does no good to say 'I told you so.' She's a dancer, and she will dance," Robert moaned. "Many dancers have danced right up until their due dates, and she thought she'd just be another lucky one. Well, she wasn't! But I swear, David, I don't know how she's going to handle this."

"How am *I* going to handle it? I've got my oral exams coming up, my baby is gone, and my wife is having a breakdown. Where do I start?" David banged his head into a wall.

Robert put his arms around the trembling young man. "My boy, you're as big a victim as she is. And all of this is falling down on you right now. Let me try and help. I'll stay with her as much as possible while you get your data cranked out. When you're ready, take your exams early and then take Gelsy away on a belated honeymoon. Get her off somewhere and maybe start all over again."

"Will she even go? She's not listening to a word I'm saying right now."

"She's hearing you, David. She's just not responding yet. Give her a little more time."

"They said she can go home tomorrow. Should I get a nurse for her?"

"No, I'll stay with her. I think a stranger in the house would just upset her more. Let me try to talk to her, maybe put a guitar in her hands and get her to sing again."

"That's a good idea, Robert. I'll arrange for an earlier test date and pour on the midnight oil, maybe get Gordie and Mark to give me a hand. Then I can be free to take her away."

"Where to? Have you thought about a destination?"

"She wanted Europe and the Grecian Isles, but I think that's too much traveling right now. Maybe just one island to relax on, not that far away. Hawaii's only a five-hour flight, and she's never been there."

"Great idea! Only plan on Kauai. That's the 'Garden Island' and the prettiest of them all."

"Kauai it is. You tell Gelsy about it. Maybe she'll listen better, coming from you."

"I'll take her home, David, and talk until I'm blue in the face. Maybe you'd better stay at the dorm a few days until she gets settled in, though."

David's face fell, but he realized that it would be too much for Gelsy to have him sleeping next to her right now. It was going to be a long, slow haul until she was ready to be a loving wife again.

"You're right, of course. I'll go and get what I'll be needing. You just get her comfortable and tell her not to worry about anything. I'll leave her alone or be there if she needs me, just tell her to let me know."

"You're a good man, David."

*****

Plip Another test tube bit the dust. How many did that make, just tonight? David had lost count, and he still had twenty pages of research notes to go through before he could take the equipment down, clean it, put it all away, and then stagger to his dorm room and get an hour or so of sleep before starting all over again.

The days had blurred into each other, and he still had no idea if he'd have the work finished in time. As for a personal life, he'd forgotten what that was. He remembered he had a wife, and it was she that would be the pot of gold at the end of this endless rainbow, but all he could see right now were the blindingly bright colors of the liquids in the test tubes that kept popping before his tired eyes.

He'd last heard of Gelsy from Robert, nearly two days ago. She was back at the house, but staying mainly in bed and refusing to answer the phone or even carry on a conversation with him. Getting her to eat was also a problem. Nothing seemed to reach her or stir her from the darkness.

The lab phone rang. David hated it when that happened; it was almost always bad news. Right now he was tempted to let it ring and have voice-mail pick it up, but he saw it was Robert's number and reached over to grab it at the last second.

"David, how are you doing? No, don't say anything . . . I can hear it in your voice. You sound pretty bad."

"Pretty bad would be an understatement, Robert."

"And I have no good news for you either, my boy. I'm so dreadfully sorry."

"What is it? Has something happened to Gelsy?!"

"No, no, nothing drastic like that. But she did finally take a phone call . . . from Naj. And you're not going to believe this, but Naj has formed his own ballet company and wants Gelsy to dance with him in New York for its opening season. It would be two weeks, with a one-week rehearsal period starting next Monday."

David leaned hard against the wall. "And she's considering it?"

"David, I hate to tell you this, but she didn't consider it. She just accepted it."

David felt the wall start to slide away from him.

"She . . . accepted?"

"Yes. She's packing right now. She's leaving tonight. She says she needs to get to New York and start taking classes to get back into shape before rehearsals start Monday."

"And when was she going to tell me about this?"

"She asked me to tell you, and I'm sorry to say, David, she asked me to drive her to the airport. She said she doesn't want to see you."

"Doesn't want . . . to see me?"

"You've got to understand, my boy. She's not herself! Gelsy would never behave like this. She has some strange idea that she sacrificed her baby to the dance. That means she must now give the rest of her life to ballet to make up for it."

David's head was swimming. "She's leaving me, Robert?"

"Please, David, I'm sure this is just a temporary delusion. Let her go for the two-week season. When it's over I'm sure she'll be back to herself. Remember when she was through with *The Nutcracker* how happy she was to be back together with you? I'm sure this will work out the same way."

David's head pounded. He closed his eyes. "Robert, I can't make it through all this if I think my wife has run out on me."

"Don't think of it like that. Just think that you're giving her time to recover from a terrible shock. You're going to be so busy during that same period of time, you wouldn't be able to spend any time with her anyway."

David slid into a chair and tried to think. Yes, that was true. Three weeks was just about how long it was going to take to get through this mess, and hopefully, he'd come out the other end with his degree. Then he could go to New York and collect his wife, and they could make a fresh start.

"OK, Robert. Tell her I want whatever is best for her right now. But I wish I could have just one look before she leaves."

"It's really better if you don't, David. She needs to focus on what she's doing."

"Tell her . . . just tell her I love her." David hung up before his voice gave out. Looking around at all the lab equipment and scattered research notes, he wondered how he could possibly wade through it all in three weeks.

*****

When the plane arrived, the last person Gelsy expected to see at the airport was Naj, but there he was, with roses and about twenty reporters hot on his heels. "Ms. Grandwood, is it true you've returned to New York to star in the new Nadinsky ballet company?" "Gelsy, sweetie, smile over here, please!" "Mr. Nadinsky, isn't it true you've always considered Ms. Grandwood to be your perfect partner?"

Gelsy found herself swept into Naj's town car and chauffeured to her hotel with a furious description—mostly in French—of every ballet she'd be dancing during the new season. For the first time since the miscarriage, Gelsy found herself laughing and being transported out of the black depression she'd been blindly stumbling in. She was a dancer again. She had a place to perform.

For his part, Naj could not have been happier. It was a terrible thing to lose a child, of course, but anything that would bring Gelsy back to him was counted as a miracle. He thought that husband of hers had walked away with her for the last time, but amazingly, here she was!

When they reached the hotel, he could hardly bear to part with her.

"*Cherie*, tell me, really, you fine, *oui*?"

"Yes, Naj, *oui*. I'm fine. Only out of shape. Let me take class, and on Monday I'll be ready for you."

"I have to be sure. I also care for you, *cherie*."

Gelsy just looked down at his hand on hers and smiled; then she slipped out of the car like a shadow. He watched her take just one suitcase into the lobby and signaled for the driver to take him home, thinking how much he wished he could take her home with him.

*****

From his golden Russian curly mop to his incredibly elegant feet Naj Nadinsky was a handsome man, no doubt about it. Slightly undersized, he stood at about five foot nine or ten on a tall day, but every facet of his body was so perfect that despairing of his height seemed silly. Already he had given pleasure to many of the most famous women in the world, but he would have gladly traded his entire list of conquests in for just one name—Gelsy.

In the beginning, she looked like another adorable young girl in the summer program, more talented than most and small enough for him to partner with ease, but still only a diversion. As they worked together, he realized her talent went far beyond any of the other budding ballerinas. She had the rare combination of musical sense, physical fluidity, and emotional response that made for a truly great dancer. Looking at the rehearsal videotapes, he could see they complimented each other perfectly. He decided in an instant that he must have her for a partner.

Unfortunately, when he went to make this offer he found she had already left for the West Coast. She had made a sudden decision, they told him, to return to California and take a freshman year at the university where her parents were on faculty. Never had Naj felt so betrayed and thwarted!

A last-ditch attempt to connect with her by partnering her in a school benefit production was terminated when she announced her engagement, with her wedding coming soon after the accident that nearly ended her dance career. Now it was like the merry-go-round was giving him one last chance at the brass ring, and he wasn't going to miss it this time. After the way he'd fought to partner her during the run of *The Nutcracker* it had become much more personal, and seeing her coming from the plane today made him realize why. He was in love with her.

"Sam-*mee*," he asked his driver and confidant, a tiny, bald black man, "what you think? Do we have chance with pretty young girl?"

"Boss!" The deep, booming voice sounded strange coming from such a small body. "I think this time she may be up for grabs. Nothing can break up a marriage like losing a baby—same thing happened to my sister and her husband. She didn't even want to look at him afterward. I think if you play your cards right, you'll get that little honey."

"And if I do, I will marry her myself. Stay on the road, Sam-*mee* . . . that's right! I said, I'll marry that little honey, as you call her. A man should settle down someday."

"Yeah, Boss, but I never expected to hear that come from *you*."

CHAPTER 11

And how did Gelsy think of David during this time?

She didn't, because as she told Robert, thinking of him made her think of the baby she lost.

"Let me try to explain it to you the way I pieced it together from all the things she said, bit by bit," Robert said to David as they worked side by side in the lab. "She always considered the greatest gift you gave her was your DNA, because she said the other women you'd slept with had been prostitutes while you were in the army. You always used protection with them, so you left no trace of yourself. Gelsy was the first woman you ever touched intimately, and she considered that was a sacred bond. But losing your child was like a sign she was unworthy of carrying your DNA. Does this make any sense?"

David froze in place. His desperately tired face looked like it was trying to grasp a principle in an equation. "Yes, Robert. It makes perfect sense, knowing her the way I do."

"Oh, I'm so glad."

"But it breaks my heart, because I don't know how to convince her she's wrong."

"Let time work its magic, my boy. I think dancing might just make her healthy again."

"As long as it doesn't make her healthy, and Naj's property! She might just decide she can't bring herself to come back to me, Robert. What do I do then?"

"You still have the crucifix, my boy. Take it out every day . . . and pray."

*****

Monday's rehearsals were barely over when Naj cornered Gelsy and insisted they have dinner together to "discuss the work." Gelsy said she'd be delighted. They could order room service and eat in her hotel suite. Naj nearly took a step back, so surprised he could only nod and smile.

So began an evening ritual of the couple meeting for dinner in Gelsy's hotel room, discussing the day's work, Naj trying very hard to make himself as irresistible as possible, Gelsy resisting him and finally sending him home so she could sleep unmolested, and Naj going home a seething, smoldering wreck of a man.

And the reporters stationed outside Gelsy's hotel were recording every late-evening soiree. The opening of Naj's new company was being heralded as the beginning of a romantic as well as a professional partnership: "This Time He's Got Her!"

Back in California, Robert took great care that David saw and heard nothing of this.

Remembering the disaster in Zurich, he enlisted Gordie and Mark's aid in keeping him from any news reports and anything that looked like a gossipmonger. His oral exams were on the horizon, and nothing was, at this point, more important.

"Have you actually talked to Gelsy about this?" Gordie whispered to Robert over a tray of samples one morning.

"Yes, last night. She just laughs and says they discuss the day's work . . . the ballets, the other dancers, where the company will go next, that kind of thing." Robert looked doubtful.

"But you don't entirely believe her?"

"Frankly, I don't know what to believe anymore, Gordie. This isn't my little girl anymore. She talks like a New Yorker now, like a professional dancer."

"Does she even mention David?"

"Never. And if I mention him, she changes the subject quickly."

"My god, don't tell him that, Robert. It would kill him. He's just hanging on, thinking that if he can make it through these next few weeks he can put a 'Dr.' in front of his name, fly back to New York, and collect his wife!"

"Don't you think I know that? And I don't know what to say when he asks if she has any messages for him, Gordie. I just make up something from the news of the day."

"The season opens tomorrow, and it will be all over the news. There's no way we can keep him from hearing about it, Robert."

Robert groaned and hung over the sink. Gordie rushed to him. "Are you OK, man?"

"Just completely worn out, Gordie. Losing Donnie and Adele was bad enough, but losing Gelsy like this is breaking my heart."

"But you're the one who keeps telling us it's just temporary, that she's coming back!"

With Gordie's help Robert eased into a chair. "The truth is, I don't know anymore, Gordie. I feel sometimes like I'm talking to a total stranger. David is my son now, and I feel closer to him, even though I've barely known him a year."

"Well, you and David share biochemistry. There's no way you can really understand Gelsy's world of ballet, even though you've been going to her recitals all these years. To her it's like a religion. I know because my sister is the same way."

"You're a very bright lad, Gordie, and I'm darned lucky to have you. I know you were disappointed when David walked in out of nowhere and made off with all the things you wanted, like the TA position . . . and Gelsy herself. That must have been hard for you to bear, but you stayed my friend and you became David's, as well. It takes a special kind of person to do that."

"Stop feeding me sweets, Robert," said Gordie, grinning, "or I'll expect to see Gelsy to come tiptoeing through the door in her Sugarplum Fairy costume! Let's get back to work."

*****

Gelsy wasn't herself, and Gelsy knew that better than anyone. For the first time since she was a child, she turned her life completely over to the world of ballet. It was so easy to do. Here she felt safe. Work yourself to the bone every day, allow yourself to relax a little in the evening over a little wine (or quite a bit of wine) with dinner, and then sleep the sleep of the dead and wake up and do it all over again. No time for bad memories, no time for any memories. Just remembering which dance step comes next.

And in the evening over wine and dinner, if Naj became more familiar, what of it? He was gentle. He never pushed her like Rennie did. And he helped make up for the aching void left by the absence of Davey.

Davey! She couldn't even let herself think of the name. Once in her head she had to banish it by quickly switching to a new ballet and counting out the steps. Then she would put Naj in her thoughts as her partner and slowly let the image of him erase everything else. Soon it became easier. Naj loved her.

After dinner they would sit on the sofa in her suite and watch TV over a bottle of wine. Naj had gone from sitting chastely on the farthest end of the sofa to sitting next to her, often nearly pulling her into his lap. His arm was around her, and his hands swept through her hair, fondled her shoulder, and worked their way down to her waist until she finally had to pull herself away.

But it was getting harder to avoid his caresses, because they could be so very sweet. Naj was skilled in pleasing a woman. Any of his ex-mistresses would tell you that time spent in his bed made for some of the best memories of their lives. And now he pulled out every stop in order to please Gelsy. His objective was simple . . . he wanted to make her his wife.

"Please, Naj, let's not speak of this. You know how it makes me feel."

"But, *cherie*, at least speak to me in French. We both understand so much better."

"And that's why I use English. I prefer not to understand you when you speak to me like this."

Looking out from his angels-nest cluster of golden curls, the good-looking young man could hardly believe his ears. All his best gestures, moves, and lines had been for nothing. Gelsy was sitting close to him but was in reality on the other side of the sofa.

"My dearest love, tell me what I can do to prove to you I am sincere? That is all I ask."

"You can leave me alone, Naj. That is *all* I ask."

"Do you wish me to continue coming here for dinner?"

"Perhaps not. Your manager told my costume assistant that he has to have prostitutes on speed dial for you after every meal with me. And it frightens him because they tell him you refuse to use protection."

The Russian jumped to his feet with a snarl. "He is out of a job, that one! I will not have a confidant who gossips."

"I wouldn't be so fast to fire him, Naj. He's been with you the whole time you've been in America, and he knows much too much about you. Let's just say it's better to keep him close."

Outmatched by this logic, Naj pursed his lips together, gave a low whistle, and then groaned. "You are no doubt right, Gelsy. I have been very indiscreet. I am so sorry."

"You have nothing to be sorry for, Naj. I'm sorry I couldn't be all you wanted me to be—partner and woman."

"It is your husband, then. He is still in your thoughts."

"No, it's not . . . that. Please understand, I have no heart for loving right now. You gave me an opportunity to work, Naj, and that's exactly what I needed. Working hard has kept me sane since I came back to New York, and I thank you. But your company opens its season in two days, and we need to concentrate everything we have on that."

"As always, I bow to your better judgment, my love. I am here with you when there are so many last-minute details I should be attending to. I will go. Let me just kiss your hand, *cherie.*"

When he was gone the quiet was overwhelming.

CHAPTER 12

David sat at the little table with a glass of wine and a cookie the size of a pancake in front of him. When his orals were over and he'd been excused from the room, instead of waiting for the outcome, he'd walked out of the building and down the block to this bistro. Sitting down at an outdoor table he'd ordered one of their famous homemade chocolate-chip cookies and a glass of Chablis and was now working his way around the pancake, breaking off pieces and stuffing them in his mouth. He tried to remember when it was he ate last, but he had no clear memory. Somebody had brought him a submarine sandwich a few days ago, but his heartburn got the better of him and he could barely touch it. Actually, he thought morbidly, he might have to go into the restaurant's restroom and heave after washing the cookie down with the Chablis, now that he thought about it. Oh well . . .

And suddenly Robert was there.

"My boy, I've been looking high and low for you!" He threw himself into an empty seat. "What do you mean by taking off like that? Didn't you know that it's protocol to stay and thank the professors for giving their time to sit for your oral exams?"

"Figured they were going to flunk me, and I'd look like an idiot thanking them for that, Robert," David replied. "Is that what you've come to tell me?"

"No, Son . . . and I say that with great pride. You have passed your orals and are now *Dr.* David Chaveral. So what do you think of that?"

The young man's head dropped down to his chest, and his hand nearly knocked over the glass of wine. Robert saved it just in time and held it up to toast him. "Here's to *two* Dr. Chaverals at one table!"

David's eyes opened wide and took in the bearded professor who had been responsible for all this. "Robert, I . . ."

"Don't say anything right now, Son. You did what you had to do. Now there's the most important thing in your life, and that's your wife. You need to go to Gelsy and bring her home."

"How can I? According to you, the season has been a big hit, and she's racking up all kinds of fantastic reviews. And I heard Gordie talking to Mark when they thought I'd left the lab, Robert. You weren't going to tell me about her and Naj spending every evening together?"

"I remembered how upset you got over Felipe, and how it all turned out to be over nothing. I can't believe after all this time she's turned to Naj after trying so hard of stay out of his reach."

"Gordie thinks it's different this time, that he really loves her, and that was the reason for this company. He wanted to get his own troupe so he could make her the prima ballerina."

"Gordie hears a lot about the dance world through his sisters, but a lot of it is just stage-door gossip. Everybody in ballet has been waiting for Naj and Gelsy to get together, ever since they first danced together at last summer's student workshop."

"Maybe they're right, Robert. Maybe they belong together, birds of a feather and all that. What is she doing with me, a biochemist, anyway?"

"I beg your pardon, but she has been partially raised by a biochemist—*me*! And she seems to be none the worse for it. Besides that, you know in your heart she loves you. If you doubt it, pull out that gold crucifix. I can't ever see her giving that to Naj."

David's hand had automatically gone to that spot on his shirt that covered the gold crucifix Gelsy had given him after they'd first made love. It was all he had to hold onto right now. And when he was alone at night, he could put his lips against the spot where Gelsy had kissed it when she blessed it for him. Robert was right. He wanted her back now so very badly.

"Will you call her tonight after the performance tonight, Robert? Will you tell her I passed my orals . . . see what she says?"

"I will, Son, but don't be surprised if she doesn't respond the way you want her to. She's tried to cut you out of her heart because you remind her that she failed as a mother to your child."

"My god, what can I do to make her see she means more to me than that?"

"You can give her time and space, but never stop being there for her. She'll get tired of running away eventually."

*****

Every day when Gelsy returned to her hotel room she hoped he'd be there, as he was after the last *Nutcracker* performance . . . when he'd arrived at the hotel while she was dancing and demanded a key to her room. Every day she entered her suite to find it as empty as it had been when she left that morning.

As usual, today the phone message light was blinking. There were usually messages from reporters, Robert, Gordie, or other friends. Some were coming to New York and wanted tickets to see the company, some just wanted to touch bases and see how she was doing. One of these messages was from a man with a gruff voice, saying, "Girl, if you want to see me, go out your door and turn right. Knock on the door next to yours. That's where I am." And the message ended with a *click*.

Next door. He was next door, right now.

But she didn't go out the door and turn right, although several times that evening she went to the wall next to the door and pressed her ear against it, trying to hear some sound from the adjoining room. Once she even pressed her entire body against the wall and willed herself to walk through it. But she didn't go knock on the door. Finally she went to bed and tried to sleep, wondering if he was waiting for her.

In the morning she forced herself to walk straight to the elevator. It was a matinee day, and she'd get to the theatre early to warm up. In between performances she stayed in her dressing room, wondering if he would come to see either show. If he did, would he come backstage? But no one came to ask permission to bring an audience member to her dressing room.

She asked Naj to have dinner with her again. Why did she do that? And why did she make sure they spoke in animated, raised voices outside her room as she fumbled with the key? No one came to the other door, and there were no more messages.

After dinner, Naj settled himself on the sofa and turned on the TV, opening another bottle of wine and motioning for Gelsy to bring over fresh glasses. This hadn't been part of her plan. Now that he was here she desperately wanted him gone, but she didn't know how to go about it. Pleading a headache wasn't her style, and she was a very bad liar, anyway. She decided to tell the truth.

"Naj, I'm so sorry. I was wrong to ask you over tonight. I don't know what I was thinking. If I made you think I've changed my mind about us, forgive me . . . I haven't."

"*Cherie*, are you asking me to go?" Naj looked dreadfully sad, and it broke her heart.

"Yes, dear boy, I am. But I am so sorry."

Without a word he stood, took her hand and kissed it, looked deep into her eyes, and then turned and walked out the door. She knew he'd never come back; his Russian pride had been cut down for the final time.

And still she didn't walk out into the hall and knock on the door next to hers.

One more matinee day and the season was over.

*****

Again Gelsy rose and dressed early, leaving her suite without even a look at the door next to hers. When she got to the stage door, she was greeted by a bevy of autograph-seekers. Today was the last day of the season, and it had been heavily advertised. Many people truly believed the final performance would end with a curtain call to end all curtain calls—Naj on one knee, offering Gelsy a diamond ring. No one knew how this rumor got started, but it had spread like wildfire and now tickets to that performance were being scalped on the street for hundreds of dollars above the original prices.

The matinee went smoothly, almost too smoothly. Naj appeared when he was supposed to, but otherwise kept himself aloof from Gelsy. People whispered that it was to make the proposal that evening even more spectacular.

The evening show began well. The first ballet on the program was for the full company without either one of the stars. The second and last ballet had Naj and Gelsy joining the company halfway through and then gradually taking over the stage until the dance turned into a pas de deux. Now they were in that last part of the last ballet, and the unimaginable happened. Gelsy ran from across the stage, launched herself into the air, . . . and Naj wasn't there.

Unexplainably, Naj was standing too far upstage with his back turned to the girl hurtling through the air. He didn't seem to notice her until she landed with a *thud* that matched the audience's cries of horror, and her body slumped to within a few inches of his left foot. Then he was on his knees, screaming. The curtain was unceremoniously lowered, and the audience seemed to not know what to do.

All except one very tall man in the orchestra seating. He climbed out of his row onto the lip of the stage, rolled under the curtain before anyone could restrain him, and was now kneeling next to the very still body of his wife.

*****

The security guards at the hospital had their hands full, trying to keep the hysterical Russian dancer from plowing through their barricade and rushing up to the emergency care unit. Orders were he was to be kept out at any cost, so said her husband, her doctor, and the godfather who was frantically trying to make plane connections from Los Angeles.

But Naj refused to leave. Reporters and photographers were having a field day, documenting his pathetic attempts to reach his beloved partner.

"A mistake in the music," he groaned. "A chord played at the wrong time. It tells me, 'Look at audience'!" And the sad truth was that he was telling the truth. A chord played out of sequence landed on his incredibly sensitive Russian ears and commanded him to turn and face downstage.

He didn't see Gelsy prepare for the jump.

"Not our problem, mister," the head security guard growled. "We've got the word to keep you clear of her, and that's what we'll do. Now, why don't you just go home like a good boy and phone the desk in the morning for news?"

Naj's manager helped him to his feet and past the platoon of newsmen to his waiting town car. The main object of their inquiry being gone, the reporters settled in to await Gelsy's godfather, just now flying in from California.

Meanwhile, David sat by the side of her bed, holding her limp little hand and waiting for the results of tests run nearly an hour ago. In all that time there hadn't been any spontaneous movement from the bed or a single sound from the tightly pursed lips. She looked exactly as she'd looked as she lay on the stage floor, like a bird that had flown into a window at high speed.

Finally a doctor came in, clutching a clipboard bristling with test results. "We have some word, Mr. Chaveral, but what we have isn't very encouraging. There's a concussion, of course. She landed with full force on her head, so that's to be expected. The question is, what will it develop into from this point? Actually, doing nothing right now is the best course of action. If we monitor her progress but don't interfere with nature's work, sometimes it's better."

"What, you mean you're not going to *do* anything for her?" David was half out of his mind. She looked so close to death, much closer than she had even after the car accident.

"If we see pressure building, we'll take action, sir. But until then we need to trust your wife's own body to mend itself. She's young and very strong."

"Looks fragile, but tough as nails," muttered David.

"What did you say, sir?

"Oh, something her godfather and I always say about her. How she looks fragile but she's really very tough."

"Yes, you've got it right. I've worked with dancers before, and they never cease to amaze me. Such tiny bodies but the strength and determination of tigers!"

David smiled. "Yes, that's Gelsy, Doctor. Maybe you're right. She bounced back from a car accident that would have left most people in a wheelchair for life. I should have more faith in her."

"Well, that was another test result I needed to discuss with you. The fall reinjured some of the places damaged by the car accident. The leg that was broken re-fractured. Not a bad break, but more than a stress fracture. And the ribs are broken, so is her left forearm. She put her arm out to stop her fall, evidently."

David's head had dropped to his chest during this description of injuries. "Oh, damn, why can't I take all those for her? She has enough to do to recover from the head injury," he whispered hoarsely.

"Give us twenty-four hours, and let's see if she's made any progress in that time." The doctor clamped a reassuring hand on David's shoulder and was gone.

But after twenty-four hours Gelsy was still unconscious.

*****

David stood over Gelsy as Robert held her hand. "So there's been absolutely no change?"

"None," David muttered, looking like an old man. "This is how she looked, lying on the floor of the stage, Robert. And there's been nothing—not the flicker of an eyelash, not a twitch—nothing since then."

"My poor boy, you've been through too much with this girl, haven't you?"

"You'd think so, but then the nurse goes and hands me this," he said and pulled a gold chain from his pocket with something hanging from it.

"What is that?" Robert asked, astonished.

"Her engagement ring and wedding ring. She had them pinned inside her costume. They had to cut it off her when they brought her in, but the nurse noticed the chain and unpinned it for me."

"Good Lord, David. All this time, she's been dancing with her rings inside her costumes?"

"How do you think that makes me feel, Robert? She must have been wearing them the whole time she was with Naj, too."

"But you said she didn't try to come see you, even when you left a message that you were right next door."

"I can only guess she was waiting for the season to be over, or that she was waiting for me to come to her. That's what I was going to do after the last performance. I was there to see if Naj really did propose to her during the curtain call, and what she'd do if he did. If she accepted, I'd have turned around, gone back to the hotel, packed, and left. If she turned him down, I would have stormed my way into her dressing room, if I had to."

"My boy, you do love her. It puts me to shame. I've been angry with her lately because she seemed to be drifting so far away from the little girl I've always known and loved. It's been hard for me to realize she went through such a terrible time, emotionally, losing the baby."

"I can't change any of that, Robert. All I can do is let her know I love her as much as I ever did, and I'll always be here for her."

Robert turned his attention back to the comatose girl. "We may not be as lucky as last time, David. She's had more than a bump on the head. There's worry about traumatic brain injury this time, you know."

David's face turned a deeper shade of grey. "Don't you think I know that? I'm praying, begging God to give her back to me, just like I did before. She's been through enough, damn it—she didn't need this! Damn Naj, anyway."

"The papers all say it really wasn't his fault. The orchestra played the wrong cue music, and he didn't see her prepare for the jump. What did you see?"

"I saw her run away from him and get ready to jump, and just then he turned to the audience. But she didn't see it. She was already halfway across the stage. It could have been either way, I guess. He could have 'arranged' for it to happen like that, because he knew if he proposed she'd refuse, or it might have been an accident. I guess we'll never really know."

"The point is, the damage is done." Robert shook his head mournfully. "We just have to wait it out, now."

And they did. Day after long, tedious day. Others offered to help, but Robert and David insisted on spelling only each other—one of them had to be on hand if she woke up. And nearly a week went by like this with no change.

It was David's watch, and he was so dreadfully tired. Although he and Robert had been given a room next to

Gelsy's, he hadn't been able to sleep more than an hour at a time. The loudspeaker would constantly blare out nurse's instructions and emergency codes even in the dead of night. Always he would wake up immediately and listen to see if they gave out her room number.

Today Robert had stumbled off to bed at the end of his shift, more dead than alive. David was beginning to worry about Robert and had already put in a call to their doctor back home. When Gelsy was last in the hospital, Robert had also ended up in the room next door, but as a patient. A heart attack caused by the loss of her parents had nearly drained him of the will to live. Now, as then, Gelsy was all that connected him to this world.

David sat and held the thin, white hand, stroking each finger carefully. The nurse had clipped her nails and filed them, "so, if she wakes, she won't scratch herself." That had made David smile. *If only she would wake* . . . wait, was that a motion in the hand? Did one of her fingers tighten on his hand or was that just wishful thinking? David sat up straighter and put his other hand underneath. With both hands he explored the long, white fingers, and then . . . there it was again! Her index finger was trying to tighten, trying to hold onto him. He tried not to get too excited; he just stroked her hand and started saying things to her, like, "I'm here, girl," and "I love you so much, Gelsy." Now her whole hand was fluttering, and it seemed to him that she was actively listening to his voice. He couldn't wait any longer. He pushed the call button and rang for the nurse.

"Get the doctor, I think she's trying to wake up," he told the nurse when she arrived. In less time than he thought possible the doctor was standing next to him, and he was showing how the fingers were trying to grip onto his hand. In a minute, Gelsy's lips pursed as if she was trying to speak, but the eyes hadn't opened yet.

"She's coming around, no doubt," the doctor said, with as much satisfaction as if he had arranged the time and date himself. "Should we alert our Professor Chaveral, or let him sleep?"

David was always amused that even in a New York hospital they'd stumbled across an ex-student of Robert's. "No, Doc, he'll want to know right away. Could you tell him? I don't want to let go of my girl's hand."

The doctor quickly exited, only to reappear in less than a minute, followed by Robert.

"Is it true, David? Is she really waking up?"

"She's trying to hold onto my hand, and she looks like she's trying to speak, Robert. Why don't you talk to her?"

Robert leaned over the bed and whispered lovingly to his godchild, "My dearest Gelsy, I'm right here, and I'm so anxious to see you open your eyes and talk to us!"

A tiny flicker of a smile brushed over her face, and David felt her squeeze his hand in a way that left no doubt. "She heard you, Robert! We're getting her back!"

*****

Another week had passed, and the hand squeezes had become more direct, the movements of the mouth were more pronounced, but still the eyes stayed closed and no words were spoken. Robert and David were sleeping better at night but still locked into their daily routine of standing guard over her bedside, and soon Robert would have to leave to return to his teaching position. David's position would be put on hold until the fall quarter.

The night before Robert was to leave David was once again completely drained of energy. Not being able to get outdoors and exercise, living on hospital cafeteria food went against his normally healthy lifestyle. Standing by the bed he knew he couldn't stand there much longer.

Neither could he sit in that hard chair. His only other option was to sleep on the floor, but from there he couldn't see if her eyes opened or if she made a move. Suddenly, all he wanted was to be next to her. *I can't hurt her if I just lie on the edge of the bed*, he thought. *We slept together like that when she was in the hospital before.*

Very carefully he made sure there were no tubes or wires in the way, and he inched himself up onto the mattress. Once he was up, he reached behind and pulled up the guardrail so he could lean back as far as possible and face her without rolling over on her. It felt so good just to lie there, watching her breathe next to him again. Like being together in bed again . . .

He drifted off and dreamed of being in the hospital and seeing a white spider crawling on a web. Then he realized the web was a guardrail and the spider was a thin hand with long white fingers. He reached up to touch it, and it closed over his hand. Then he had pulled himself to his knees and found himself looking into Gelsy's eyes . . . *just like now*, he thought with no room for doubt. His hand reached out for her hand, and he was looking into her eyes, wide open and full of questions.

"Yes, you're in the hospital. Yes, you're going to be all right. Robert is next door. I'll go get him in a minute if you want. I should call for the doctor first, though," he explained and reached for the button.

As she'd done before, she made him stop. How, he wasn't sure—she didn't speak or move her hand but the impulse from her to wait until they'd had more time together was unmistakable.

"What is it, Gelsy?"

Her eyes dropped down to her left hand. She tried to stretch out her fingers . . . "Is it your hand, girl?" She looked back at him, then back to her hand. Suddenly an image came into his head as if she was transmitting it to him. "Your rings? Is that what you want?"

The look was so completely happy it was obvious he'd said the right thing. Lowering the guardrail he rolled off the bed, retrieved his jacket, and pulled out the chain with the rings attached. "I've kept them safe for you, Gelsy. I just didn't know if you were going to want them back or not."

The look she gave would have melted a much harder heart. As it was it sent David free-falling in space. He slipped the chain around her neck and laid the rings out where she could see them. "Because your fingers are so thin right now, I'm afraid they won't stay on." Then he called for the doctor.

"Well, hello, young lady! It is nice to finally meet you. I'm Dr. Wood, and I'm an old student of your godfather's. Professor Chaveral is right next door, and as soon as I check a few vital signs we'll bring him over to welcome you back."

Gelsy managed a brief smile for the doctor, which pleased him no end. While he was checking her, David slipped next door to wake Robert up with a "Want to say 'hi' to your godchild?"

Luckily, the doctor had about finished his vitals because once Robert entered the room and saw Gelsy's eyes open and saw her smile at him, he was nearly out of control. He hung over her bed, holding her hand and telling her how very happy he was, over and over. The doctor finally ordered him back to bed with a shot to help him sleep for his own health, promising him his godchild wouldn't run away in the meantime.

David stayed. Still exhausted, he sat in the hard chair and waited for the doctor to finish up; then he crawled back onto the edge of the bed next to his wife, pulled up the guardrail, put her hand up to his lips, and kissed her fingers. He told her to get some sleep and promptly dozed off himself. Did she sleep? Yes, but not until she lay still for a very long time, looking at her husband and thinking how much she had missed him.

*****

They were going back home together. Gelsy was stable enough to be moved on a medical flight. Robert and David would fly commercial practically alongside of her all the way to the West Coast. At first David was uncertain about being parted from her for the five-and-a-half-hour trip, but Robert assured him she was in good hands. Dr. Wood was riding with her and wouldn't leave until she was settled at UCSM Medical Center, and they'd all reunite on the tarmac of LAX as soon as they touched down. Even so, it was a stressful flight for the young husband, worried all the way that the medical evacuation plane might crash and he would find himself on the tarmac alone.

But the flights were both uneventful, and David was relieved to be reunited with his wife at the airport. An ambulance was ready to take her to the medical center, so all they needed to do was hop into the car Gordie and Mark had thoughtfully parked for them in the LAX parking lot and follow it to UCSM. After getting Gelsy settled in her new room it was getting late, so the two men kissed her good-night and headed home together.

"My god! It seems like years since I've been in this house," Robert said as he unlocked the front door.

"You? How about *me?*" groaned David, walking in and immediately slumping into an easy chair.

"We definitely need some sleep, Son. Gordie said he left some microwaveable food in the freezer, so why don't you heat something up and then head directly to bed?"

"Sounds like a plan, Robert."

After a little food and a hot shower, David felt more human than he'd felt in weeks. He slipped into a clean pair of pajamas and headed for bed.

The bed. For over a minute he just stood and looked at it. He'd never had to sleep alone in it before; always there was Gelsy. Usually he'd lie there and watch her get ready, then hold out his arms to her when she came to turn back the covers. How could he possible sleep there without her?

Robert was an early riser and required coffee by six o'clock, no later. On his way to the kitchen he nearly stumbled across a pile of blankets cascading off a living room sofa where David was sprawled, sound asleep.

CHAPTER 13

She smiled; she held his hand, but she didn't speak or move her legs. The days went by with no visible improvement, and David began to worry. *Was she going to recover?* Dr. Wood had told him to let time heal her, but time seemed to be going by so quickly, and he missed her so much.

Whenever he could, he'd try to lie alongside her in the hospital bed. She begged him with her eyes to do this, and it was what he wanted most. Just to be as close to her as possible, just to look into her eyes as he spoke to her and see that she was understanding him, then to feel the pressure of her hand . . . it was enough for the moment.

The room was constantly filled with flowers. All Gelsy's friends, fans, and most of all, Naj, were sending flowers to brighten her long road to recovery. Naj hadn't tried to see her again since that first night. Knowing David was keeping guard at her bedside had kept him away at first, and then he took his new ballet company on a tour of Europe. David was not sad to see him go.

"So Gordie and Mark have been running all the research and teaching all the classes for almost a month, Gelsy. You should see them now! They think they're entitled to tenure any day, and I'm voting for them. I don't know what we would have done without them. But they said they did it for you as much as for Robert or me. I have to say, those guys really love you, girl. I'd be jealous if I didn't already have a ring on your finger. Oh, well, around your neck right now." Here he paused to tug playfully on the gold chain. "When you're well, let's have that real church wedding we talked about, then go on a real honeymoon. How does that sound?" And her eyes glistened with tears she blinked back.

"Goo . . . goo . . . goo . . . od. Goo . . . od. Good," she stuttered, in a whisper.

"Oh my god, girl—you're talking! The doc was right. All you needed was time. Maybe it will take a while longer, I don't care. I'll wait for you forever, Gelsy. Just come back to me as much as you can." David kissed her fingertips over and over, but she jerked her hand toward her face and he saw her purse her lips. Slowly and carefully he bent over and kissed her on the mouth, her lips feeling as soft and yearning for his as they always had. "Oh, girl, I can feel you coming back, all right. Just don't let that Baptist doctor catch us in bed together making out, OK?"

But it wasn't the doctor who came striding through the door at that very moment; it was Robert. Catching them in a compromising position made his day, and he collapsed into a chair in perfect fits of laughter.

"I am telling on you two." He chortled. "You know how strict they are around here. Canoodling in a patient's bed is enough to get you barred from the premises for life, my boy!" And he went off into another bout of hysterical laughter, because Gelsy had unmistakably mouthed "Shut *up*!" at him.

The three of them had a happy family evening that night, the first carefree evening they'd enjoyed in over a month. After Robert left, David crawled back up onto the bed and again tried to hold Gelsy as close as possible. It was beginning to sink in how very long it had been since he was this close to her. After becoming used to being married to her and sleeping beside her every night, it was a terrible feeling to lie in a bed alone again. He had no idea how lonely he could be.

"Gelsy, if the doctors say it's OK, do you think we could take you home pretty soon? Maybe get a hospital bed installed at the house, if that's what you need, and get in-home nurses. We could fix the bathroom on the first floor so you could get into it easier. What do you think?"

And if hand squeezes and eye blinks count as "yes," then she answered in the positive most enthusiastically.

*****

Another month went by. Gelsy was at home, but in a hospital bed on the first floor, David slept on a sofa alongside the bed or occasionally on the bed itself. Sleeping on the bed was problematic, though, because it made him desire her. The cast was off her leg, and the re-fractured area had mended well. All the other various tubes and needles had been removed because Gelsy was conscious and could swallow medication quite nicely on her own. The area where the concussion had occurred would have to be watched, of course, but time and soon some physical therapy should strengthen her weakened body. As it was, there had been very little voluntary movement from the chest down. This worried David. When she was injured before, she'd recovered movement in her legs almost immediately.

"Is she going to be able to walk again, or dance?" he kept asking the doctors.

"Only time will tell," they'd tell him, over and over. But time was going by so quickly, and still she lay so still, while the nurses worried about bed sores.

One evening he came home early to find the nurse giving her a bath in the new hydro-lift they'd installed in the first-floor bathroom. He helped lift her out of the warm water and dry her. Her bath had revitalized her; she was giggling like a schoolgirl. After they got her into a clean nightgown and into a freshly made bed, David told the nurse she could go home early. Then he stood over the bed and just looked at her for a long minute before reaching for her hand. She looked into his eyes and mouthed the words "I love you," and he felt as if he'd been struck down by lightning. Clenching his jaws and trying not to squeeze her hand too hard, he crawled up onto the bed and eased himself carefully next to her body.

When he was right up against her, he kissed her over and over, running his hand first over the fabric of the nightie and then pulling it up to reach underneath. Putting his hand on her bare skin after so long was like being given water when you're in the desert. He couldn't believe anything could feel so good. She'd lost weight, of course, but her smooth skin and the various areas he found so fascinating were there under his fingers. Once again he felt the electricity of needing her. *I don't think I can stop. What am I going to do?* he thought frantically. His fingers felt for the soft fur of the little woodland creature that lived between her thighs. He found it, and then he felt the muscles of her thighs quiver under his touch. Slowly, she opened her legs slightly to allow him access to her body.

She moved because she wanted him! He nearly lost his mind. Suppose Robert came home and caught them having sex on the hospital bed? He was just going to have to take that chance.

Unzipping his pants and sliding them down, he pressed himself up against her. For several minutes he only did this while opening and touching her with his hand, until she was completely ready and breathing hard. Then he moved himself into position and entered her as gently as possible. She looked at first deep into his eyes; then she shut her eyelids tight and moaned. The sound sent him reeling . . .

he was pleasing her! My god! How long had it been since they had pleased each other like this? But this was what the term "making love" really meant, pleasing the one you love.

They clung together as closely as possible, and he moved as slowly and carefully as he could, but the weeks of being without her had left him so hungry he couldn't stop himself from exploding with a groan that sounded like it was torn out of his chest. He was afraid to look at her at first, but when he did, she was smiling happily. Then he heard Robert's car pull up in the driveway.

By the time Robert walked in, David was sitting in the chair, and Gelsy was decently covered up, except for a big smile that nearly split her face apart. "My goodness, David. Have you been telling her dirty jokes? She looks like she just heard a good one!"

That was too much for Gelsy. She opened her mouth and began to laugh in gasping sounds that almost sounded like sobs, but came closer to speech that anything they'd heard from her yet. Robert was astounded, while David just hoped he wouldn't inquire any further into what might have caused this sudden turn of events.

Later that night, with Robert snoring loudly in the background, the two lovers repeated their union, this time slower and with a little less restraint. David was getting the feeling that Gelsy's body was not hurting, just waking up after a long sleep. Making love was a way for her to get back in touch with the different parts that had seemed so scattered and out of her reach.

Afterward they lay together, kissing and with him telling her over and over how very much he loved her. Having her back again in his arms, he swore he'd never let her go again. He said he didn't want to live one day thinking she didn't love him any longer. For her part, she nuzzled him gently and then whispered, "No, no." He thought his heart would break with joy.

In the morning, when the nurse came to give Gelsy the morning medications and ministrations, she let out a whoop of delight. Calling the two men into the room, she had Gelsy demonstrate for them how she was suddenly wiggling her legs and arms.

It was slow. *Nothing like the miraculous first recovery*, thought Robert as he watched David lifting Gelsy in his arms and carrying her out to the patio. But she was definitely recovering at last, and for that he was grateful. Sitting out on the patio on a Friday night and playing his guitar for her, singing the old songs he and her father had sung from the time she was a child helped Gelsy to take heart and she began to bloom again. Every week brought her closer to normalcy. First her speech returned; then there was more controlled movement in her hands and arms so she could feed herself. The legs were the most stubborn. Although they gained mobility, they didn't have the strength yet to support her body. But still, she was well enough to do away with the hospital bed and move back into her own room upstairs. David happily carried her wherever she needed to go.

David knew Robert would assume they had resumed marital relations as they were together again in her old bedroom, although they never spoke of it. One day, during lunch in the university's faculty dining room, David himself skirted the issue saying, "I think we should talk to the doctor about starting her on birth control pills again."

Robert stopped chewing on his sandwich for a moment, took a gulp, and said, "My boy, are you telling me you've been doing nothing about that?"

"Well, I thought with her as badly injured as she was—"

"What? That she couldn't get pregnant?!" Robert looked around hastily and leaned in, lowering his voice. "Have you noticed how she's been positively blooming lately, and that she's put on weight?"

"Well, yes. She's getting better, thank God."

"David, she might be—"

"No, Robert!"

"You need to go out and buy some tests at the drugstore on your way home tonight. You know, the kind she used with the little sticks."

"*No*, Robert!"

"*Yes*, David. You will do that because you have been damned careless. How could you?"

On his way home from work, David took a bus to an area of town where he was pretty sure he wouldn't see anyone he knew; he looked both ways before diving into a drugstore and came out with a neat bag of little boxes. He boarded a bus headed to his home and tried to imagine explaining the bag and what it contained to Gelsy that evening.

*****

As it turned out, there was no need for the kits. Gelsy had just started her period that morning. David heaved a huge sigh of relief and called the doctor's office about the prescription.

Now the spring quarter was getting ready to turn into summer intersession, and everywhere on campus preparations were being made for graduation events. "You realize," Robert informed them both over breakfast, "David will be expected to walk in the biochem's ceremonies and be hooded."

"Be 'hooded,' Robert?" David looked a little confused.

"That's university lingo for when they put the little satin banner-thing around your shoulders and then say, 'Congratulations, Dr. Chaveral,'" Gelsy told him with great relish. "How delightful, Buba! I get to see my husband officially get his doctorate degree! I can hardly wait."

David had been at the point of asking if it was really necessary, since he had actually graduated at winter quarter, but seeing the excited look on her face scotched that idea. Anything that made her that happy was worth doing. Then an idea struck him, and he leaned over the table.

"How's this for a plan . . . we top off the graduation with a Church wedding and a real honeymoon?"

Gelsy's eyes opened wide. "But I can't walk yet."

"There's lots of ways to work around that, and you've worn your rings around your neck long enough. You're gaining weight every day and looking like your old self. By then you can wear them on your hand without being afraid of losing them. What do you say?"

"What do I say? Oh, Buba, help me here! What can I say?!"

David stood up, walked to Gelsy's chair, and slowly sank down to one knee. Taking her hand in his, he looked into her eyes and said, "Giselle Marie Grandwood Chaveral, I love you with all my heart. I'm asking you to please remarry me and go on a long, romantic honeymoon with me."

"Oh, my dear Davey, I would love that . . . if you don't think I'll be too much trouble."

He stood and kissed her on the forehead. "You'll be no trouble, girl. It will be pure joy to carry you in my arms around a tropical island."

Robert stood and gave them both a hug. "All right, then it's settled. We can start making the wedding plans tonight. But right now David and I have to go out and work for a living, my sweet. Say good-bye to your husband so I can take him off to the salt mines."

"Good-bye to both my handsome men. I will see you this evening. Have a good day, and be sure to give Gordie and Mark my love."

"Will do. You have your physical therapy today?" David leaned over for one last kiss.

"Yes, and the nurse will drive me."

When they were gone, Gelsy turned to the nurse and asked, "Anna, could we possibly go early to the physical therapy center?"

*****

The box on the top shelf held her mother's wedding gown. "There's a little stepladder behind the door . . . no, on the other side, in back," Gelsy instructed the new nurse. "That's it! Just put the box in my lap. Oh, wonderful—it hasn't yellowed at all. I haven't seen it since I was about fourteen. Here, Anna, help me stand and don't let anyone see me."

Gelsy struggled to her feet with the nurse's aide and held the dress against her body, looking in the mirror on the back of the door. "Yes, I think I can wear it without any alterations. It was meant to be a little loose and flowy, you know, being in that medieval style. Oh, yes, it is rather like my Juliet dress!"

"What about a veil?" asked the delighted little nurse.

"My mother didn't wear one, just flowers in her hair like I did in the chapel. But I'm thinking a veil would be nice."

"I'm calling my sister right now and having her bring over her veil. It is the most beautiful veil anybody has ever seen, and we can try it on with the dress to see how you like it."

"What a wonderful idea!"

The nurse grabbed the phone, and Gelsy began to struggle out of her clothes. Amazingly enough, it took less than twenty minutes before the nurse and her sister had her standing on her own again, this time wearing the dress with a fingertip-length tulle veil that floated like a piece of smoke around her shoulders.

"I don't know what to say . . ." Tears were threatening to drown Gelsy's shaky smile.

"I do," the nurse replied firmly. "The most beautiful thing I've ever seen in my life. Sorry, Frieda," she said, addressing her sister, "but she looks even better in it than you did."

"I'll be the last one to argue with you there, honey," Frieda shot back good-naturedly. "Considering she's the size of an eel, and I'm more like a walrus! No, you obviously should wear it, Gelsy. It can be your 'something borrowed,' you know."

"I can't thank you enough for the veil, all the help . . . and for keeping my secret."

"You can invite us to the wedding, honey," Frieda exclaimed with a big hug.

Later that evening when the three family members were alone together, going over the wedding plans, Gelsy told them, "It's all set. I'm wearing Mama's wedding dress and borrowing a veil from Anna's sister."

Robert was out of his seat in a flash. "My dearest girl," he exclaimed and flung himself at her neck. "I can't wait to see you in the dress your mother wore at her wedding! You'd better expect me to get a little teary, though. And since I'm the troubadour for the event, I might get a bit of a frog in my throat, but if I do just remember I did back then, too."

He hugged and kissed her until she laughingly pushed him away from the wheelchair with "Enough, Buba! You'll make Davey jealous."

That night, after David had carried her up the stairs and settled her in bed, she asked, "Is this going to be enough for you, my dear? Suppose I never do get any better?"

David sat on the edge of the bed and simply looked at her. "Girl, I won't lie. It kills me that you can't walk or dance like you used to, but it's mainly for your sake. I can't imagine how you'll be happy living like this the rest of your life, no matter what I do to try and make up for it. But for my part, Gelsy, I just want you in my life. I guess I'm totally selfish in that way. Whatever it takes, I just want you here with me."

"And I'm sorry to have put you through so much, my darling. I promise from now on to be perfectly healthy— no more hospitals! We won't have to worry about somebody catching us in bed together anymore."

"That suits me just fine. Let me take a quick shower and I'll join you."

Lying there, waiting for him and listening to the shower run, Gelsy tentatively lifted one leg under the covers and then the other. First just an inch or two, then several inches, then both legs at the same time, making the bedding form a tent-like structure. Suddenly she heard a gasp.

"Davey! I hear the water running. I thought you were in the shower!"

"I came back for my pajamas. Gelsy, are you lifting your legs?"

"Oh, sweetheart, I wanted to surprise you."

"You sure as hell did that. Wait a second." He turned off the water and came back to the edge of the bed. "Do that again, please?"

Slowly she lifted both legs in the air, held them a few seconds, and lowered them again. "Don't tell Buba, Davey. I wanted it to be a surprise on the wedding day. Gordie and Mark will come and help me walk like they did before, but I will not be married in a wheelchair!"

"My strong, stubborn, beautiful girl." David held her so tight she could barely breathe. "I'm so proud of you. And Robert will be, too. He'll be flabbergasted!"

"I feel like all of this has been my fault, darling. I wanted a child too soon. I wasn't ready to give up my dancing for its safety. Then I ran away from my failure and from you and tried to lose myself dancing with Naj, and even letting him fawn over me a little, because it made me feel special. Then I jumped that night without making sure first that he was prepared to catch me. Everything was my fault. I've been a stupid little girl who needed to grow up."

"*My* girl, because that's what you are. Not stupid, ever—just human. God, how I love you!"

"And I wanted to go to your hotel room, darling. I just couldn't until my contract with Naj was finished, and I could come to you free. Does that make sense?"

"Yes, but you had me worried that you might be thinking of staying with him, after all."

"Never. There is only one man in the world for me. That sounds like a tired, old saying, but it happens to be true. Since the first day we were together, I can see no one else." She pulled him down beside her and caressed his face.

"So if I make you my bride at the altar of the cathedral, maybe I can start feeling less afraid of losing you every time you're out of my sight for five minutes?" He took her hand and kissed it.

"I will walk to meet you at the altar of the cathedral to make you happy, Davey, but in my heart I can be no more married to you than I was in the hospital chapel."

David looked at her thoughtfully. "Are you saying you'd rather just skip the big wedding?"

"No, darling, I look forward to wearing my mother's wedding gown, and so many of our friends who couldn't be at the chapel can come this time. No, we must go through with it!"

"I'm glad. Just one question—are we inviting Naj?"

"We can invite him, and he can send a polite apology. The company will be dancing in Australia, and it's rather a long journey." She giggled. "Maybe he'll send a microwave."

"Which we'll donate to charity!" David muttered. "How about Rennie?"

"Rennie is in a national touring company, playing Lord-knows-where. No, I think we can safely leave him and his sisters off the list."

"Wow, I'm batting a perfect score here. All the ex-boyfriends safely out of the way," he teased her by pulling her hair. "Unless you want to count Felipe?"

"The company is also touring in Canada. And, by the way, he and Antonio have started letting themselves be seen together in public. So far there has been very little talk. People are more open-minded now, and most don't seem to care."

"Well, I'm glad for them both. Being in love myself, I just want everyone else to be happy."

CHAPTER 14

The morning was perfect for an outdoor graduation ceremony. For once everything was on time, and the ten o'clock starting time actually coincided with the opening notes of "Pomp and Circumstance" from the university orchestra. This ceremony was for only the graduate students of the biology and chemistry departments, but the audience first had to wait through the master's candidates before the doctoral degrees were handed out. When David's name was called, a round of applause broke out against all instructions not to applaud individual students. His proud dad, wife, and buddies were just too excited to hold themselves back. And when the stole was placed around his broad shoulders and the presenter shook his hand and said, "Congratulations, *Dr.* David Chaveral," Gelsy sat in her wheelchair and started to weep with sheer joy.

Afterward, there were lots of pictures taken and backslapping from everyone in the department; then it was off to a restaurant where Robert had reserved the banquet room for a festive lunch.

After lunch, everyone took a few hours to rest and change clothes before meeting again at the Cathedral of the Angels. Everything had been set up in advance, and all they had to do was take their places, David stepping out in front of the altar only slightly nervous. *Piece of cake*, he thought. *I've done this before.* Gordie and Mark accompanied him out, but then they walked by him and continued walking down the side aisle. At the back of the church he saw them making a chair out of their arms and lifting a vision in white. Gently they set her on her feet in the center aisle and took her arms on both sides, slowly walking her to meet David. But he couldn't recognize this apparition. Dressed in a medieval-style sheer white gown covered in lace, her head and shoulders were covered in a translucent shimmering veil that hung from a crown of pearls set in her beautifully braided hair. She might have been the spirit of a saint, too glorious to be human. His heart nearly burst when he thought to himself, *this is my beloved wife.*

Robert had been playing "The Wedding Song," and when he first caught sight of Gelsy, he faltered and choked up, but, as he said later, it was exactly at the same place where he'd choked up at her mother's wedding march. As David and Gelsy knelt together before the altar, he was very glad Gelsy had made him put tissues in his pocket.

Their vows exchanged and rings symbolically given (David had never for a moment taken his wedding ring off), the time came for the groom to kiss the bride. In order to do so, David had to lift the fingertip veil and push it back, but somehow he got lost in the gathered tulle and Gordie's two sisters, Victoria and Luisa, serving as bridesmaids, had to laughingly step in to help him find his bride's face to kiss.

Once he found it, he knew exactly what to do. Remembering the moment in the north parking lot when she'd first kissed him on the cheek, he took her face in his hands and brought her lips up to his. As the guests rose in a standing ovation, David scooped his bride up in his arms, and, ignoring her protestations that she could walk, he strode up the cathedral aisle carrying her with the look of a man who had found the finish line and won the race.